# It was still raining...

Dr. Galbraith saw Leonora's bedraggled figure ahead of him, marching briskly along, Wilkins beside her. He passed them, pulled into the side of the road, opened the door and said, "Get in—I'm going past your place. Your dog can sit in the back."

"Good morning, Doctor," said Leonora pointedly. "Please don't bother. We are both very wet. We shall spoil your car."

He didn't answer, but got out of the car and walked around to where she stood. "Get in," he said pleasantly. He glanced at her. "A waste of time, Leonora...."

"What's a waste of time?"

"Trying to get the better of me."

**Betty Neels** spent her childhood and youth in Devonshire, England, before training as a nurse and midwife. She was an army nursing sister during the war, married a Dutchman and subsequently lived in Holland for fourteen years. She lives with her husband in Dorset, and has a daughter and grandson. Her hobbies are reading, animals, old buildings and writing. Betty started to write upon retirement from nursing, incited by a lady in a library bemoaning the lack of romantic novels.

## Books by Betty Neels

# The Daughter of the Manor
## Betty Neels

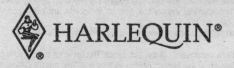

HARLEQUIN®

TORONTO • NEW YORK • LONDON
AMSTERDAM • PARIS • SYDNEY • HAMBURG
STOCKHOLM • ATHENS • TOKYO • MILAN • MADRID
PRAGUE • WARSAW • BUDAPEST • AUCKLAND

ISBN 0-373-03583-7

THE DAUGHTER OF THE MANOR

First North American Publication 2000.

Copyright © 1997 by Betty Neels.

This edition published by arrangement with Harlequin Books S.A.

Visit us at www.romance.net

Printed in U.S.A.

# CHAPTER ONE

THE village of Pont Magna, tucked into a fold of the Mendip Hills, was having its share of February weather. Sleet, icy rain, a biting wind and a sharp frost had culminated in lanes and roads like skating rinks, so that the girl making her way to the village trod with care.

She was a tall girl with a pretty face, quantities of dark hair bundled into a woolly cap, her splendid proportions hidden under an elderly tweed coat, and she was wearing stout wellies—suitable wear for the weather but hardly glamorous.

The lane curved ahead of her and she looked up sharply as a car rounded it, so that she didn't see the ridge of frozen earth underfoot, stumbled, lost her footing and sat down with undignified suddenness.

The car slowed, came to a halt and the driver got out, heaved her onto her feet without effort and remarked mildly, 'You should look where you're going.'

'Of course I was looking where I was going.' The girl pulled her cap straight. 'You had no business coming round that corner so quietly...'

She tugged at her coat, frowning as various painful areas about her person made themselves felt.

'Can I give you a lift?'

She sensed his amusement and pointed out coldly, 'You're going the opposite way.' She added, 'You're a stranger here?'

'Er-yes.'

Although she waited he had no more to say; he only

stood there looking down at her, so she said matter-of-factly, 'Well, thank you for stopping. Goodbye.'

When he didn't answer she looked at him and found him smiling. He was good-looking—more than that, handsome—with a splendid nose, a firm mouth and very blue eyes. She found their gaze disconcerting.

'I'm sorry if I was rude. I was taken by surprise.'

'Just as I have been,' he replied.

An apt remark, she reflected as she walked away from him, but somehow it sounded as though he had meant something quite different. When she reached the bend in the lane she looked back. He was still standing there, watching her.

Pont Magna wasn't a large village; it had a green, a church much too big for it, a main street wherein was the Village Stores and post office, pleasant cottages facing each other, a by-lane or two leading to other cottages and half a dozen larger houses—the vicarage, old Captain Morris's house at the far end of the street, and several comfortable dwellings belonging to retired couples. A quiet place in quiet countryside, with Wells to the south and Frome to the east and Bath to the north.

Its rural surroundings were dotted by farms and wide fields. Since the village was off a main road tourists seldom found their way there, and at this time of the year the village might just as well have been a hundred miles from anywhere. It had a cheerful life of its own; people were sociable, titbits of gossip were shared, and, since it was the only place to meet, they were shared in Mrs Pike's shop.

There were several ladies there now, standing with their baskets over their arms, listening to that lady—a stout, cheerful body with a great deal of frizzy grey hair and small, shrewd eyes.

'Took bad, sudden, like!' she exclaimed. 'Well, we all knew he was going to retire, didn't we, and there'd be a new doctor? All arranged, wasn't it? I seen 'im when 'e came to look the place over. 'Andsome too.' She gave a chuckle. 'There'll be a lot of lady patients for 'im, wanting to take a look. Lovely motor car too.'

She beamed round her audience. 'Would never 'ave seen 'im myself if I 'adn't been coming back from Wells and stopped off to get me pills at Dr Fleming's. There 'e was, a great chap. I reckon 'e'll be taking over smartish, like, now Dr Fleming's took bad and gone to 'ospital.'

This interesting bit of news was mulled over while various purchases were made, but finally the last customer went, leaving Mrs Pike to stack tins of baked beans and rearrange packets of biscuits. She turned from this boring job as the door opened.

'Miss Leonora—walked, 'ave you? And it's real nasty underfoot. You could 'ave phoned and Jim could 'ave fetched whatever you wanted up to the house later.'

The girl pulled off her cap and allowed a tangle of curly hair to escape. 'Morning, Mrs Pike. I felt like a walk even though it's beastly weather. Mother wants one or two things—an excuse to get out...'

I'm not surprised, thought Mrs Pike; poor young lady stuck up there in that great gloomy house with her mum and dad, and that young man of hers hardly ever there. She ought to be out dancing.

She said out loud, 'Let me have your list, miss, and I'll put it together. Try one of them apples while you're waiting. Let's hope this weather gives over so's we can get out and about. That Mr Beamish of yours coming for the weekend, is 'e?'

'Well, I shouldn't think so unless the roads get better.'

The girl twiddled the solitaire diamond on her finger and just for a moment looked unhappy. But only for a moment. 'I dare say we shall have a glorious spring...'

Mrs Pike, weighing cheese, glanced up. 'Getting wed then?' she wanted to know.

Leonora smiled. Mrs Pike was the village gossip but she wasn't malicious, and although she passed on any titbits she might have gleaned she never embellished them. She was a nice old thing and Leonora had known her for almost all of her life.

'We haven't decided, Mrs Pike.'

'I like a nice Easter wedding meself,' said Mrs Pike. 'Married on Easter Monday, we were—lovely day it was too.' She gave a chuckle. 'Poor as church mice we were too. Not that that matters.'

It would matter to Tony, reflected Leonora; he was something in the City, making money and intent on making still more. To Leonora, who had been brought up surrounded by valuable but shabby things in an old house rapidly falling into disrepair, and who was in the habit of counting every penny twice, this seemed both clever and rather daunting, for it seemed to take up so much of Tony's life. Even on his rare visits to her home he brought a briefcase with him and was constantly interrupted by his phone.

She had protested mildly from time to time and he had told her not to fuss, that he needed to keep in touch with the markets. 'I'll be a millionaire—a multimillionare,' he told her. 'You should be grateful, darling—think of all the lovely clothes you'll be able to buy.'

Looking down at her tweed skirt and wellies, she supposed that her lack of pretty clothes sometimes irked him and she wondered what he saw in her to love enough to want to marry her. The family name, perhaps—they had

no hereditary title but the name was old and respected—
and there was still the house and the land around it. Her
father would never part with either.

It was a thought which scared her but which she
quickly dismissed as nonsense. Tony loved her, she wore
his ring, they would marry and set up house together. It
was a bit vague at present but she hoped they wouldn't
have to live in London; he had a flat there which she
had never seen but which he assured her he would give
up when they married. And he had told her that when
they were married he would put her home back on its
original footing.

When she had protested that her father might not allow that, he had explained patiently that he would be
one of the family and surely her father would permit
him to see to it that the house and land were kept as
their home should be. 'After all,' he had pointed out to
her, 'it will eventually be the home of our son—your
parents' grandson...'

She had never mentioned that to either her mother or
her father. How like Tony, she thought lovingly—so
generous and caring, ready to spend his money on restoring her home...

Mrs Pike's voice interrupted her thoughts. 'Pink
salmon or the red, Miss Leonora?'

'Oh, the pink, Mrs Pike—fishcakes, you know.'

Mrs Pike nodded. 'Very tasty they are too.' Like the
rest of the village she knew how hard up the Crosby
family were. There never had been much money and Sir
William had lost almost all of what had been left in some
City financial disaster. A crying shame, but what a good
thing that Miss Leonora's young man had plenty of
money.

She put the groceries into a carrier bag and watched

Leonora make her way down the icy street. She had pushed her hair back under her cap and really, from the back, she looked like a tramp. Only when you could see her face, thought Mrs Pike, did you know she wasn't anything of the sort.

Leonora went into the house through one of the side doors. There were several of these; the house, its oldest part very old indeed, had been added to in more prosperous times and, although from the front it presented a solid Georgian façade with imposing doors and large windows, round the back, where succeeding generations had added a room here, a passage there, a flight of unnecessary stairs, windows of all shapes and sizes, there were additional doors through which these various places could be reached.

The door Leonora entered led through to a gloomy, rather damp passage to the kitchen—a vast room housing a dresser of gigantic proportions, a scrubbed table capable of seating a dozen persons, an assortment of cupboards, and rows of shelves carrying pots and pans. There was a dog snoozing before the Aga stove but he got up, shook himself and came to meet her as she put her bag on the table.

She bent to fondle him, assuring him that no doubt the butcher's van would be round and there would be a bone for him. 'And as soon as it's a bit warmer we'll go for a real walk,' she promised him. He was an old dog, a Labrador, and a quick walk in the small park at the back of the house was all that he could manage in bad weather.

The door on the other side of the kitchen opened and a short, stout woman came in, followed by a tabby cat, and Leonora turned to smile at her.

'It's beastly out, Nanny. I'll take Wilkins into the garden for a quick run.' She glanced at the clock. 'I'll see to lunch when I get back.'

Nanny nodded. She had a nice cosy face, pink-cheeked and wrinkled, and grey hair in a tidy bun. 'I'll finish upstairs. I've taken in the coffee—it's hot on the Aga when you get in.'

Wilkins didn't much care for the weather but he trotted obediently down one of the paths to where a door in the brick wall opened onto the park—quite a modest park with a small stream running along its boundary and clumps of trees here and there. They went as far as the stream and then turned thankfully for home.

The house was a hotchpotch of uneven roofs and unmatched windows at the back but it had a certain charm, even in winter months. Of course many of its rooms were shut up now, but Leonora conceded that if you didn't look too closely at peeled paint and cracks it was quite imposing. She loved it, every crack and broken tile, every damp wall and creaking floorboard.

Back in the kitchen once more, Wilkins, paws wiped and his elderly person towelled warm, subsided before the Aga again, and Leonora hung her coat on a hook near the door, exchanged her wellies for a pair of scuffed slippers and set about getting lunch—soup, already simmering on the stove, a cheese soufflé and cheese and biscuits.

Carrying a tray of china and silver to the dining room, she shivered as she went along the passage from the kitchen. It would be sensible to have their meals in the kitchen, but her mother and father wouldn't hear of it even though the dining room was as cold as the passage, if not colder.

'Mustn't lower our standards,' her father had said when she had suggested it. So presently they sat down to lunch at an elegantly laid table, supping soup which had already been cooling by the time it got to the dining room. As for the soufflé, Leonora ran from the oven to the table, remembering to slow down at the dining-room door, and set it gently on the table for her mother to serve, thankful that it hadn't sunk in its dish.

'Delicious,' pronounced Lady Crosby. 'You are such a good cook, darling.' She sighed faintly, remembering the days when there had been a cook in the kitchen and a manservant to wait at table. What a blessing it was that Leonora was so splendid at organising the household and keeping things running smoothly.

Lady Crosby, a charming and sweet-tempered woman who managed to avoid doing anything as long as there was someone else to do it, reflected comfortably that her daughter would make a good wife for Tony—such a good man, who had already hinted that once they were married he would see to it that there would be someone to take Leonora's place in the house. She was a lucky girl.

She glanced at her daughter and frowned; it was unfortunate, but Leonora was looking shabby.

'Haven't you got anything else to wear other than that skirt and sweater, dear?' she asked.

'Well, Mother, it's awful outside—no weather to dress up. Besides, I promised Nanny I'd help her with the kitchen cupboards this afternoon.'

Her father looked up. 'Why can't that woman who comes up from the village see to them?'

Leonora forbore from telling him that Mrs Pinch hadn't been coming for a month or more. Her wages had been a constant if small drain on the household purse, and when her husband had broken an arm at work she had decided to give up her charring and Leonora had seen the chance to save a pound or two by working a bit harder herself.

She said now, 'Well, Father, I like to go through the stores myself once in a while.' A remark which dispelled any faint doubts her parents might have had.

'Do wear gloves, dear,' observed her mother. 'Remember it's the Willoughbys' dinner party this evening—your hands, you know!'

The Willoughbys lived just outside the village in a small Georgian house in beautiful grounds, and since they had plenty of money it was beautifully maintained. They were elderly, good-natured and hospitable and Leonora enjoyed going there.

The cupboards dealt with, she got tea with Nanny and carried the tray through to the drawing room. Even on a cold winter's day it looked beautiful, with its tall windows, plaster ceiling and vast fireplace in which burned a log fire that was quite inadequate to warm the room. The furniture was beautiful too, polished lovingly, the shabby upholstery brushed and repaired.

Her mother was playing patience and her father was sitting at a table by the window, writing. She set the tray down on a small table near her mother's chair and went to put more logs on the fire.

'I thought we might give a small dinner party quite soon,' observed Lady Crosby. 'We owe several, don't we? You might start planning a menu, darling.'

'How many?' asked Leonora, humouring her parent, wondering where the money was to come from. Dinner parties cost money. They could pawn the silver, she supposed with an inward chuckle; on the other hand she could make an enormous cottage pie and offer it to their guests...

'Oh, eight, I think, don't you? No, it would have to

be seven or nine, wouldn't it? We can't have odd numbers.'

Lady Crosby sipped her tea. 'What shall you wear this evening?'

'Oh, the blue...'

'Very nice, dear, such a pretty colour; I have always liked that dress.'

So did I, reflected Leonora, when I first had it several years ago.

Getting into it later that evening, she decided that she hated it. Indeed, it was no longer the height of fashion, but it was well cut and fitted her splendid shape exactly where it should. She added the gold chain she had had for her twenty-first birthday, slipped Tony's ring on her finger and took a last dissatisfied look at her person, wrapped herself in a velvet coat she had worn to her twenty-first-birthday dance, and went downstairs to join her parents.

Sir William was impatiently stomping up and down the hall. 'Your mother has no idea of time,' he complained. 'Go and hurry her up, will you, Leonora? I'll get the car round.'

Lady Crosby was fluttering around her bedroom looking for things—her evening bag, the special hanky which went with it, her earrings...

Leonora found the bag and the hanky, assured her mother that she was wearing the earrings and urged her down to the hall and out into the cold dark evening, while Nanny went to open the car door.

The car, an elderly Daimler which Sir William had sworn that he would never part with despite the drain on his income, was at the entrance; Leonora bundled her mother into the front seat and got into the back, where she whiled away the brief journey thinking up suitable topics of conversation to get her through dinner. She would know everyone there, of course, but it was as well to be prepared....

The Willoughbys welcomed them warmly for they had known each other for a long time. Leonora glanced round her as they went into the drawing room, seeing familiar faces, smiling and exchanging greetings; there was the vicar and his wife, old Colonel Howes and his daughter, the Merediths from the next village whose land adjoined her father's, Dr Fleming, looking ill, and his wife and, standing with them, the man in the car who had witnessed her undignified tumble.

'You haven't met our new doctor, have you, dear?' asked Mrs Willoughby, and saved Leonora the necessity of answering by adding, 'James Galbraith.' Mrs Willoughby smiled at him. 'This is Leonora Crosby—she lives at the Big House—you must come and meet her parents.'

Leonora offered a hand. Her 'How do you do?' was uttered with just the right amount of pleasant interest, but it had chilly undertones.

His hand was large and cool and firm and she felt compelled to look at him. Very handsome, she conceded—rather sleepy blue eyes and very fair hair, a splendid nose and a rather thin mouth. He was tall too, which was nice, she reflected; so often she found herself looking down on people from her five feet ten inches. Now she had to look up, quite a long way too!

'Six foot four?' she wondered out loud.

The Flemings had turned away to speak to someone else. Dr Galbraith's mouth quivered faintly. 'Five, actually. Are you feeling sore?'

She said austerely, 'I hardly think that is a question I need to answer, Dr Galbraith.'

She had gone rather pink and glanced around her, on the point of making an excuse to go and talk to the vicar. She was stopped by his saying, 'I speak in my professional capacity, Miss Crosby; presumably you will be one of my patients.'

'I am never ill,' said Leonora, unknowingly tempting fate.

Mrs Willoughby had joined them again. 'Getting to know each other?' she wanted to know. 'That's nice—take Leonora in to dinner, will you, James?' She tapped his sleeve. 'You don't mind if I call you James? Though if ever I need your skill I'll be sure to call you Doctor.'

Leonora had been sipping her sherry; now she put the glass down. 'I really must circulate, and Nora Howes is dying to come and talk to you.'

He looked amused. 'Oh? How do you know that?'

'Woman's intuition.' She gave him a brief smile and crossed the room and he watched her go, thinking that a splendid creature such as she deserved a better dress.

She had been right about Nora Howes, who laid a hand on his sleeve, threw her head back and gave him an arch look. Older than Leonora, he supposed, as thin as a washboard and wearing a rather too elaborate dress for a dinner party in the country. But he could be charming when he liked and Nora relinquished him reluctantly as they went in to dinner, and he turned with relief to Leonora as the soup was served. Not a girl he could get interested in, he reflected—far too matter-of-fact and outspoken—but at least she didn't simper.

It was a round table so conversation, after a time, became more or less general. He had Mrs Fleming on his other side, a quiet middle-aged woman, a good deal younger than her husband and anxious about him.

'I didn't want him to come,' she confided quietly, 'but

he insisted. 'He's not well; he's going into hospital to-morrow.'

He said gently, 'You mustn't worry too much, Mrs Fleming. If he leads a quiet life for the next few months and keeps to his treatment he'll get a great deal better.'

She smiled at him. 'If anyone else had said that I should have supposed them to be pulling the wool over my eyes, but because it's you I believe what you've told me.'

'Thank you. I wish all patients were as trusting. Don't hesitate to call me if you're worried.'

'I won't. It's so nice that you're going to live at Buntings—such a lovely old house and it's been empty far too long.'

She turned to speak to her neighbour and presently everyone went back to the drawing room to drink coffee and gossip. It might be a small village but there was always something happening.

The party broke up shortly before eleven o'clock and since it was cold outside no one lingered to talk once they'd left the house. Sir William unlocked his car door and glanced at the Rolls-Royce parked beside him.

Who's the lucky owner? he wondered, and saw Dr Fleming getting in.

'Good Lord, Bill, have you come into a fortune?' he called.

'No, no, James owns it. Rather nice, isn't it?' He disappeared inside and Sir William got behind his wheel and backed the car. 'Lucky young devil,' he said to no one in particular. 'Come up on the pools, has he?'

Leonora made some vague reply. She was thinking about Tony. She hadn't seen him for a week or so; perhaps he would come at the weekend. She hoped so; she felt strangely unsettled and just seeing him would reassure her—she wasn't sure why she wanted to be reassured, but that didn't matter; Tony would set her world to rights again.

He did come, driving up on Saturday afternoon in his Porsche, and if his kiss and hug were lacking the fervour of a man in love she didn't notice because she was glad to see him.

He went indoors with her to meet her parents and make himself agreeable and then they went for a walk. He took her arm and talked and she listened happily to his plans. They would marry—he was a bit vague as to exactly when—and he would set about restoring her father's house. 'There's a chap I know who knows exactly what needs to be done. It'll be a showplace by the time it's finished. We can have friends down for the weekend...'

Leonora raised a puzzled face. 'But Tony, we shan't be living here; Mother and Father wouldn't much like a great many people coming to stay—even for a weekend.'

He said rather too quickly, 'Oh, I'm thinking of special occasions—Christmas and birthdays and so on; it's usual for families to get together at such times.' He smiled at her. 'Tell me, what's been happening since I was last here?'

'Nothing much. The Willoughbys' dinner party, and—I almost forgot—the new doctor to take over from Dr Fleming—he had a heart attack—not a severe one but he's got to retire.'

'Someone decent, I hope. Local chap?'

'Well, no, I don't think so. I don't know where he comes from. He's bought Buntings—that nice old house at the other end of the village.'

'Has he, indeed? Must have cost him a pretty penny. Married?'

'I've no idea. Very likely, I should think. Most GPs are, aren't they?'

Tony began to talk about himself then—the wheeling and dealing he had done, the money he had made, the important men of the business world he had met. Leonora listened and thought how lucky she was to be going to marry such a clever man.

They went to church the following morning and she stood beside Tony in the family pew, guiltily aware that she was glad the new doctor was there too and could see her handsome fiancé.

Dr Galbraith was handsome too, and his height and size added to that, but he was... She pondered for a moment. Perhaps it **was** the way he dressed, in elegant, beautifully tailored clothes, sober ties and, she had no doubt, handmade shoes—whereas Tony was very much the young man about town with his waistcoats and brightly coloured ties and striped shirts. She took a peep across the aisle and encountered the doctor's eyes, and blushed as though she had spoken her thoughts out loud and he had heard her.

She looked away hastily and listened to the Colonel reading the lesson, with a look of rapt attention, not hearing a word, and she took care not to look at the doctor again.

It was impossible to avoid him at the end of the service; he was standing in the church porch with the Flemings, talking to the vicar, and there was no help for it but to introduce Tony to him.

'The new GP,' observed Tony. 'I don't suppose there's much work for you around here. Wouldn't mind your job—peace and quiet in the country and all that. You fellows don't know when you're lucky. I'm in the City myself...'

The doctor said drily, 'Indeed? One of the unlucky ones? You must be glad to spend the weekend in this peaceful spot.'

Tony laughed. 'Not even a weekend—I must go back after lunch, try and catch up with the work, you know.'

'Ah, well, it's a pleasant run up to town. I dare say we shall meet again when next you're here.' The doctor smiled pleasantly and turned away to talk to the vicar's wife, who had joined them, and presently when he and the Flemings left the little group he did no more than nod affably at Leonora, who gave him a decidedly chilly smile.

'A bit of a stiff neck, isn't he?' asked Tony as they walked back to the house. He gave his rather loud laugh. 'I don't need to have qualms about the two of you!'

'If that's a joke,' said Leonora, 'I don't think it's funny. And why do you have to go back after lunch?'

'Darling—' he was at his most cajoling '—I simply must. There's no let-up, you know, not in my world— the business world. Keeping one step ahead is vital...'

'Vital for what?'

'Making money, of course. Don't bother your pretty head; just leave it to me.'

'Will it always be like this? I mean, after we're married? Will you be dashing off at all hours of the day, and do we need a lot of money? Don't you earn enough for us to get married soon?'

He gave her a quick kiss. 'What a little worrier you are. I am that old-fashioned thing—comfortably off. We could marry tomorrow and live pleasantly, but I don't want to be just comfortably off; I want to be rich, darling—a flat in town, decently furnished, money to go abroad when we want to, all the clothes you want to buy, dinner parties, the theatre. I want you to have the best of everything.'

'Tony, I don't mind about any of that. I'm not a town girl; at least, I don't think I am. I like living in the country and I don't care if we haven't much money. After all, I'm used to that.' She added thoughtfully, 'Perhaps you've fallen in love with the wrong girl...'

He flung an arm around her. 'Darling, what nonsense. The moment I set eyes on you when we met at the Willoughbys I knew you were what I was looking for.'

Which was quite true—she was a very pretty girl, had been ready to fall in love, and was an only child, with no large family to complicate matters. She lived in a lovely old house with plenty of land, which would be worth a fortune once he could get his hands on it.

He would have to go slowly, of course, and naturally he couldn't do anything to make Leonora unhappy. Her parents would be just as happy in a smaller house, somewhere close by, and he and Leonora could live in the big house. It would be a splendid focal point for meeting influential men and their wives—men who would give him a helping hand up the financial ladder.

Decently dressed, Leonora would prove an asset; she had lovely manners and a delightful voice. A bit outspoken at times and a good deal more intelligent than he had expected, but he was sure that he could persuade her to his way of thinking.

It was a couple of days later when Leonora met the doctor again. The icy weather had become quite mild and it rained from a dull sky. Sir William had caught cold and sat morosely by the fire, while his wife fussed around him and Nanny offered hot drinks and aspirin, which left Leonora looking after the household and doing the shopping, for, much as she loved her father, she could see that two females hovering over him was just about as much as he could stand. So she made the beds and hoovered and did most of the cooking and now they were running out of groceries.

In a mackintosh even older than the tweed coat, a hat, shapeless with age, rammed down onto her head, she picked up her basket, announced that she was going to the village and, accompanied by Wilkins, set out.

'At least we won't skid on ice,' she observed to Wilkins, who was plodding along beside her. 'Though we are going to get very wet.'

Mrs Pike's shop was empty, which was a good thing for she allowed Wilkins to come in out of the rain, offering a sheet of newspaper which he was to sit on while Leonora took out her list.

A visit to Mrs Pike's was a leisurely affair unless she had a great many customers; she chatted while she collected bacon, cheese, the loaf the baker left each day, the marmalade Sir William preferred, tea and coffee, sugar and flour. Not that there was much to gossip about: Mrs Hick's new baby, the Kemp's youngest boy with a broken arm—'What do you expect from boys, anyway?' asked Mrs Pike—and Farmer Jenkins making a bit of trouble about his milk quota. 'Whatever that is, Miss Leonora; I'm sure I don't know what the world's coming to!'

This was one of Mrs Pike's frequent observations and the preliminary to a lengthy monologue of a gloomy nature, so it was a relief when two more customers came in together and Leonora was able to gather up her shopping and start for home.

It was still raining. Dr Galbraith, driving out of the village, saw Leonora's bedraggled figure ahead of him, marching along briskly, Wilkins beside her. He passed them and then pulled in to the side of the road, opened the door and said, 'Get in—I'm going past your place. Your dog can sit at the back.'

'Good morning, Doctor,' said Leonora pointedly. 'Please don't bother. We are both very wet; we shall spoil your car.'

He didn't answer but got out of the car and walked round to where she stood. 'Get in,' he said pleasantly, and opened the door for Wilkins, who was only too glad to get out of the rain.

'Oh, well, all right,' said Leonora ungraciously, and slid into the front of the car. 'I have warned you that we are both very wet.'

'Indeed you have, and now I'm wet as well.' He glanced at her. 'A waste of time, Leonora...'

'What's a waste of time?'

'Trying to get the better of me.' He was driving now and turned to smile at her. 'How are your mother and father?'

'They're very well—no, that's not quite true. Father's got a very bad cold; he's a shocking patient when he's not well and Mother gets worried.'

'In that case, perhaps it might be as well if I took a look at him. An antibiotic might get him back on his feet—colds can drag on at this time of year.'

'Yes, but aren't you on your rounds or something?'

'No.' He swept the car through the gates and up the neglected drive to the front door and got out to go round the bonnet and open her door and then free Wilkins.

'Do come in,' said Leonora, all at once minding her manners, 'and take off your coat. I'll fetch Mother.' She turned round as Nanny came down the staircase.

'Oh, good, here's Nanny. This is Dr Galbraith, our new doctor; he's kindly come to see Father.'

Nanny eyed the doctor. 'And that's a mercy. How do you do, Doctor? And a fine, well-set-up young man you are, to be sure. Give me the coat; I'll dry it out while Miss Leonora takes you to see the master.'

She turned her attention to Leonora then. 'And you too, Miss Leonora—off with that coat and that old hat and I'll give Wilkins a good rub down. There'll be coffee when you come down.'

Dismissed, the pair of them went upstairs to find her father sitting in a chair by a brisk fire with his wife bending over him. She looked up as they went in and gave a relieved sigh. 'Dr Galbraith, I was wondering if I should ask you to call. You met Leonora...'

'Yes, Lady Crosby, and it seemed sensible to take a look at Sir William, since I was passing.' He went to look at his patient and Leonora discovered that he was no longer a man who persisted in annoying her but an impersonal doctor with his head stuffed full of knowledge, and to be trusted. His quiet voice and his, 'Well, sir, may I take a look at you?' was reassuring.

# CHAPTER TWO

SIR WILLIAM coughed, blew his nose, coughed again and
spoke.

'Nothing much wrong—just this infernal cold—cough
keeps me awake, makes me tired.'

Leonora helped him off with his dressing gown and
followed her mother to the door. She paused to ask, 'Do
you need me to stay?'

She was surprised when the doctor said, 'Please,' in
an absent-minded voice as he bent over his patient.

She stood by the window and glanced out at the rain-
sodden landscape, listening to the doctor's quiet voice
and her father's querulous answers. He wasn't well; perhaps they should have called the doctor sooner, she
thought worriedly.

She loved her parents and got on well with them; indeed, she had been perfectly happy to stay home with
them. Before her father had lost his money, there had
been plans afoot to send her to friends in Italy, sugges-
tions that she might train for a career, have a flat in
town—the world had been her oyster.

She hadn't regretted the loss of any of these, although
she sometimes longed for new clothes, a visit to the theatre, evenings out at some famous restaurant. The long-
ings weren't deep enough to make her unhappy, and now
that she and Tony were to marry it seemed to her that
she would have the best of both worlds—living with
Tony, sharing his social life, and coming home whenever she wanted to.

25

Dr Galbraith's voice disturbed her thoughts. 'If you would help your father with his dressing gown?'

He didn't look up as he wrote out a prescription. 'If you could get this made up? It's an antibiotic. And a couple of days in bed. Flu can hang around for a long time if it isn't treated promptly.'

He handed her the prescription and closed his bag. 'I'll call again in a day or so, but if you're bothered about anything don't hesitate to call me.'

'Hope I haven't given it to my wife,' observed Sir William.

'As I said, let me know if you are worried about anything.' He glanced at Leonora. 'Forewarned is forearmed.'

'Obliged to you for coming,' said Sir William. 'I'm sure there'll be coffee downstairs for you. Busy, are you?'

The doctor, who had been up all night with a premature baby, replied that no, he wasn't unduly so.

'Probably a good deal easier than a city practice,' said Sir William, blithely unaware that the doctor's practice extended for miles in every direction. Some of the outlying farms were well off the main roads, and the lanes leading to them were, as often as not, churned into muddy ruts.

Downstairs Lady Crosby was waiting for them in the drawing room, looking anxious.

'Fetch the coffee, Leonora; Nanny has it ready. Come and sit down, Doctor, and tell me if Sir William is ill or if it's just a bad cold.'

'Flu, Lady Crosby. He will need to keep to his bed for a few days and take the antibiotic I have prescribed. He should be perfectly all right within a week, provided he keeps warm and quiet; he isn't as young as he was.'

He smiled at her and she smiled back. 'Sixty-one—I'm a good deal younger.' Lady Crosby, who had been a very pretty girl, wasn't averse to a little admiration and her smile invited it.

She was disappointed and a little put out; she had been spoilt and pampered for most of her life, only during the last difficult years she had had to forgo the comforts and luxuries she had taken for granted. She loved her husband and daughter, but took their care and attention as her right. The expected compliment from the doctor wasn't forthcoming. All he said was, 'I'm going to Bath; perhaps your daughter might come with me and get the prescription I have written up for Sir William. I shall be returning within the hour and will give her a lift back.'

Leonora, coming in with the coffee, heard the last part of this and said, in her matter-of-fact way, 'Oh, there is no need for that. I can take the car—I might hold you up.'

'Nonsense, dear,' said her mother. 'Why take the car when you can get a lift? Dr Galbraith is coming back to the village. You'll probably have time to pop into that wool shop and see if you can match my embroidery silks...'

She poured the coffee. 'Have you taken a tray up to your father, dear? I dare say he would like a hot drink.' She smiled charmingly at the doctor. 'We shall take the greatest care of him, Doctor.'

He glanced from mother to daughter; Leonora had inherited her mother's good looks on a more generous scale; he fancied she had inherited her father's forthright and strong-willed nature. It was no life for a girl such as she—living with elderly parents and, he suspected, bearing the burden of the household management in the down-at-heel, still beautiful house. Still, he remembered, she was engaged; presumably she would marry shortly. Not that he had liked the man.

Leonora, wrapped up against the weather, got into the car presently. He was glad to see that she had found a decent hat and her gloves and handbag were beyond reproach. Not that he cared in the least about her appearance, but with her striking looks she deserved the right clothes.

Glancing at her profile, he set himself out to be pleasant and had the satisfaction of seeing her relax. Gradually he led the conversation round to more personal matters, putting a quiet question here and there so casually that she answered freely, unaware that she was talking about things that she had kept tucked away at the back of her head because neither her mother nor her father would want to hear about them, and nor would Tony: small niggling doubts, little worries, plans she had little hope of putting into effect.

They were on the outskirts of Bath when she said abruptly, 'I'm sorry, I must be boring you. I expect you get enough moaning from your patients.'

'No, no, talking never bores me, unless it is the kind of chat you encounter at parties. I'm going to park at the Royal National Hospital. There are several chemists in Milsom Street; fetch the prescription and come back to the car. There's a quiet restaurant by the abbey—I hope you'll take pity on me and have lunch.' When she opened her mouth to refuse he said, 'No, don't say that you have to go home at once; you would be too late for lunch anyway, and I promise you I'll get you home within the next hour or so.' He smiled suddenly. 'I have an afternoon surgery...'

'Well, that would be nice; thank you. I don't like to be away from home for very long because of Father...'

He had stopped the car by the hospital and got out to open her door. 'I'll be fifteen minutes. If I'm longer than that, go and wait in the entrance hall...'

He watched her walk away. She was just as nice to look at from the back as from the front. He smiled a little as he went into the hospital.

When she got back he was there, waiting for her. 'We'll leave the car here; it's only a few minutes' walk. You know Bath well?'

The restaurant was small, quiet, and the food was excellent. Leonora, savouring a perfectly grilled sole, thought she must remember to tell Tony about it; it was a long time since they had been out together for a meal—he was happy to stay at home with her, he always told her, and she spent hours in the kitchen conjuring up a meal he would like from as little of the housekeeping money as possible.

She wished that he were sitting opposite her now instead of Dr Galbraith and despised herself for the mean thought. After all, he had no reason to give her lunch and she had to admit he was a pleasant companion. All the same, she had the sneaking feeling that behind that bland face there was a man she wouldn't care to cross swords with.

They talked as they ate, exchanging views on Bath, Pont Magna and its inhabitants, and the various houses in it.

'I used to go to Buntings when I was a little girl,' Leonora told him. 'It's a lovely old house. Are you happy there?'

'Yes. It is the kind of place where you feel instantly at home. I expect you feel that about your own home?'

'Oh, yes. It's badly in need of repairs, though. Some rich American wanted to buy it last year, but Father wouldn't hear of it. His family have lived in it for a very long time. It would break his heart to leave.'

'I can understand that. It is a delightful house. Rather large to look after, though.'

'Yes, but quite a few rooms are shut and Nanny and I can manage the rest.'

She frowned and he said smoothly, 'Nannies are marvellous, aren't they? Shall we go? I must get you back before someone wonders where you are.'

Less than an hour later he stopped the car at her home, got out to open her door and waited until she had gone inside. He had beautiful manners, she thought, and hoped that she had thanked him with sufficient warmth.

Her mother was in the drawing room. 'There you are, dear. Have you got those pills for your father? He's rather peevish so I came down here to have a little rest— I find looking after someone ill so very tiring. We'll have tea soon, shall we? Perhaps Nanny could make a few scones.'

Leonora said, 'Yes, Mother,' and went to look for Nanny.

In the kitchen Nanny asked, 'Have you had some lunch, Miss Leonora? There's plenty of that corned beef—'

'Dr Galbraith gave me lunch, Nanny—a rather splendid one too. Mother wants tea a bit earlier—and scones? I'll come and make them, but first I must go and see about Father.'

Sir William, back in his bed, was glad to see her.

'I've got your pills and you can start them straight away,' she told him cheerfully. 'And how about a cup of tea and some of that thin bread and butter Nanny cuts so beautifully?'

She sat down on the side of the bed. 'I don't suppose

you feel like sausages for supper. How about scrambled eggs and creamed potato and jelly for pudding?'

'That sounds good.' Her father smiled at her. 'We shall be lost without you when you marry, my dear.' He paused to cough. 'You are quite sure, aren't you? Tony is a successful young man—he'll want to live in London.'

She shook her head. 'Not all the time—he was talking about coming down here whenever we could. He loves this house, you know.'

Her father said drily, 'It is a gold-mine for anyone with enough money to put it in order. As it is, it's mouldering away. At least it will be yours one day, Leonora.'

'Not for years, Father.' She got up and fetched a glass of water and watched him while he swallowed his pill. 'Every four hours,' she warned him. 'Now I'm going to get your tea.'

She dropped a kiss on his head and went down to the kitchen, where, since Nanny was making the scones, she got her father's tea-tray ready and presently bore it upstairs.

Back in the drawing room with her mother, she drew a chair closer to the fire. 'I must say that Dr Galbraith seems to be a very pleasant man. Charming manners, too. We must invite him to dinner one evening, Leonora—remind me to make a list of guests. We must think of something delicious to give them.'

Leonora said, 'Yes, Mother,' and bit into a scone. 'I dare say Father will enjoy that once he's feeling better.'

Her mother said vaguely, 'Oh, yes, of course, dear. What did you have for lunch? So kind of the doctor to give you a meal.'

When Leonora had told her she added, 'Ah, yes, I know the restaurant you mention. The food there is good but expensive. I dare say that, being a single man, he can afford such places. I'm surprised that he isn't married, but I expect he is merely waiting until he is settled in at Buntings. A doctor, especially one with a country practice, needs a wife.'

Leonora murmured an agreement, and wondered why he should need one more than a GP with a town practice.

'He would have done very well for you,' went on Lady Crosby, 'but of course you've already got a fiancé in Tony. Most suitable and such a charming man.'

Leonora thought about Tony. He was charming and fun to be with. He teased her a good deal, told her that she was old-fashioned and strait-laced. 'I'll forgive you that,' he had told her, laughing. 'You'll change once I get you up to town.'

She had pointed out that she didn't want to change. 'I wouldn't be me,' she'd told him, aware that she had irritated him. The next moment, however, he had been laughing again; perhaps she had mistaken the look on his face. They would be happy together, she felt sure; she looked at the diamond on her finger and told herself how happy she was at that very moment just thinking about him.

That night she dreamt of Dr Galbraith, and the dream persisted in staying in her head all next day. She did her best to dispel it by writing a long letter to Tony.

Her father was feeling a little better, although he was still coughing a good deal and looked tired. She wondered uneasily what would be done if the antibiotic didn't do its good work; Dr Galbraith hadn't said that he would call again...

He came the next morning and, since she was upstairs with the Hoover, it was her mother who opened the door to him.

'Dr Galbraith—how kind of you to call again. Just in time for coffee. I'll get Leonora or Nanny to bring it to the drawing room.' She smiled her charming smile. 'I do hate having it by myself...'

Any opinion the doctor might have had about this remark he kept to himself.

'I called to see Sir William and, much though I would enjoy a cup of coffee, I can't spare the time—I have quite a few visits to make this morning.' He smiled in his turn. 'If I might go up?'

'Oh, dear, we could have had a nice little chat. Do you want me to come up with you? Leonora is hoovering the bedrooms; I'm sure she'll see to anything you may want.'

The Hoover was making a good deal of noise; he had time to study Leonora's back view before she turned round. She was wearing a sensible pinny and had tied her hair in a bright scarf; the Hoover, being past its prime, tended to raise almost as much dust as it sucked up.

She switched it off when she saw him, wished him a good morning and said, 'You want to see Father? He had quite a good night but he's chesty...'

She whipped off the pinny and also the scarf and led him into her father's room.

The doctor pronounced himself satisfied with his patient but added that he would need to remain in bed for several days yet. 'Get up for an hour or so, if you wish,' he said, 'but stay in this room. I'll come and see you again in a couple of days or so.'

Going downstairs with Leonora, he observed, 'Your father is by no means out of the woods. He has escaped pneumonia by a whisker and anything other than rest and a warm room, plenty to drink and plenty of sleep is liable to trigger off a more serious condition. He'll do well if he stays where he is—don't let him get out of bed for much more than an hour or so.'

He sounded just like the family doctor, thought Leonora waspishly, but then that was exactly what he was. Did he need to be quite so impersonal, though? After all, they had had lunch together...

Her mother came into the hall as they reached it and he bade her a pleasant goodbye, added a few reassuring words about Sir William's condition, smiled briefly at Leonora and drove away, leaving her feeling vaguely unsettled.

Tony came at the weekend, breezing into the house, explaining that he had torn himself away from his work to take them by surprise.

'You look as though you need a bit of cheering up,' he told Leonora, who certainly didn't look her best after four days of coping with her irascible parent. 'How is Sir William? Not too bad, I hope?'

'He is better, but he has a bad chest; he's getting up today for a few hours but he mustn't go outside until his cough has cleared up.'

'Where is that delightful mother of yours?'

'She went to Colonel Howes' for coffee.' Leonora hesitated. 'Tony, would you mind awfully if I left you for a bit? I'll get some coffee for you and there are the morning papers in the drawing room. I haven't quite finished the bedrooms and I must make a bed for you. You are staying?'

'Well, of course, if it's too much bother...' He contrived to look hurt and she said quickly, 'No, no, of course it's not, and I shan't be long.'

'I'll go and have a chat with your father,' suggested

Tony, getting out of the chair into which he had flung himself.

'No— Oh, dear, I keep saying no, don't I? He is shaving and getting dressed. We'll both be down presently. I'll just fetch the coffee. Did you have a good trip here?'

He said sulkily, 'Not bad. It's the deuce of a long way from town, though.'

I ought to be so pleased to see him, reflected Leonora, putting china on a tray and listening to Nanny's opinion of those who came for the weekend uninvited, but he might have phoned first. 'I'll have to go to the butcher's and get some chops.' She interrupted Nanny's indignant flow. 'Have we plenty of eggs?' she asked.

'No. We have not. Mr Beamish will have bacon for his breakfast and one or two of those mushrooms Mrs Fleming sent over. The cake's almost finished too.'

'Oh, I'll make another one, Nanny—there'll be time before lunch...'

'There's the doorbell,' said Nanny in a voice which suggested that she was much too busy to answer it. So Leonora opened the door, to find Dr Galbraith towering over her. She stared up into his calm face and felt a ridiculous urge to burst into tears. She didn't say anything and presently he said placidly, 'I've come to see your father.'

'Yes, but—yes, of course. Do come in...'

'You were doing something urgent. If I'm interrupting do go and finish.' He looked her over slowly. 'You look put upon. What's the matter?'

As Tony came into the hall, the doctor said, 'Ah, yes, of course,' in a very quiet voice, and added a much louder, 'Good morning.'

'Ah, the local GP. Good morning to you. Come to check on the invalid, have you?'

'Yes.' Dr Galbraith turned towards Leonora. 'Shall we go up?'

'I'll come along too—the old chap's always glad to see me.'

The doctor was saved the necessity of answering as Nanny came into the hall with the coffee-tray.

'I'm putting your coffee in the drawing room, Mr Beamish; you'll need to drink it while it's hot.'

Tony, although he didn't like her, did as he was told, mentally promising himself that once he was married to Leonora one of the first of his acts would be to get rid of Nanny.

Going up the staircase, the doctor noted that Leonora looked less than her best; her hair was tied back and hung in something of a tangle down her back, and she was without make-up, not that that mattered for she had clear skin and a mouth which didn't need lipstick; moreover, she was wearing an elderly skirt and a sweater with the sleeves rolled up. But none of this really detracted from her undoubted good looks.

'Is Lady Crosby at home?' he asked casually.

'No, I'm sorry, but she's having coffee with the Howeses—you've met the Colonel and his daughter...'

He had dined with them on the previous evening but he didn't say so.

'Don't you care for visiting?' he wanted to know.

'Me? Oh, yes, it's nice meeting people. But today—well, the weekend, you know, and then I didn't know Tony was coming so there's a bit more to do.'

They had reached her father's door and the doctor didn't answer.

Her father was sitting in his dressing gown, looking out of the window. He turned as they went in, saying, 'Leonora? Is that my coffee? It's past ten o'clock.'

He saw the doctor then. 'Good morning. You see how much better I am. I shall get dressed presently and go downstairs for lunch.'

'Why not?' The doctor sat down beside him. 'Such a delightful view from this window even at this time of the year. How is the cough?'

'Better—much better—and I've taken those pills you left for me. Leonora sees to that, don't you, my dear?'

Leonora said, 'Yes, Father,' and admired the back of the doctor's head.

'A splendid nurse,' her father went on. 'We are indeed lucky to have a daughter who takes such good care of us both.'

'You will miss her when she marries,' observed the doctor, taking his patient's pulse.

'Yes, yes, of course, although Tony has a great liking for this house; I'm sure they will visit us as often as possible.'

The doctor didn't hurry but tapped Sir William's chest, listened to his heart, asked a number of leisurely questions and finally pronounced himself satisfied. 'Stay indoors for another day or so,' he advised, 'and when you do go out wrap up warm.'

Tony came out of the drawing room as they reached the hall.

'Well, what's the verdict? I'm not surprised that Sir William has been ill—this house may look a thing of beauty but it's riddled with damp. Needs money spent on it. More sense if he found something smaller and modern.'

Leonora gave him a surprised look. 'Tony, you know as well as I do that Father and Mother will never move. Why should we? We're happy here—it's our home.'

He took her arm. 'Darling, of course it is. Come and

have some coffee.' He nodded at Dr Galbraith. 'Nice to meet you,' he observed.

Leonora frowned. Tony was being rude. 'Thank you for coming, Doctor. I'll keep an eye on Father. You won't need to come again?'

'I think not, but do give me a ring if that cough doesn't clear up within the next week or ten days.' He shook hands, ignored Tony and went out to his car, got in and drove away.

'You were rude,' said Leonora, leading the way to the drawing room.

'Sorry, darling. I can't stand the fellow, looking down that long nose of his. Thinks he knows everything—I've met his sort before.'

'He's a good doctor,' said Leonora, 'and everyone likes him—except you.'

'Let's not argue about him. I've come to spend the weekend with you, so let's enjoy ourselves. Heaven knows, it's hard enough to get away.'

Tony had sat down again. 'How about getting into something pretty and we'll go out to lunch?'

'Tony, I'd love to, but I can't. When you got here I was making beds—and when I've done that I must get lunch and see about making a cake and getting something made for this evening. Father has to have his coffee and his lunch, and Mother will be back presently. They like their tea at half past four and dinner has to be cooked…'

'For heaven's sake, Leonora…can't Nanny deal with all that?'

'No, she can't. The kitchen has to be cleaned, food has to be prepared, she has to answer the door and Father's bell if I'm busy and one of us will have to go to the village and do some extra shopping.'

'Well, I thought I would be welcome,' said Tony sulkily, 'but it seems I'd better leave as quickly as possible!'

'Don't be silly,' said Leonora briskly. 'You know how glad I am to see you, but what's the use of pretending that I can sit here, nicely dressed and made up, when it's simply not possible? We could go for a walk in the afternoon.'

She saw his irritable frown. 'I'm sorry, Tony...'

'Let's hope that next time I manage to get here you'll be looking more like my fiancée and not the home help.' He laughed as he spoke and she laughed with him, hiding her hurt. He was delightful and charming, she told herself, and she loved him, and she reminded herself that he worked very hard and had little time to enjoy his leisure.

All the same the beds had still to be made. It was fortunate that her mother returned, delighted at the sight of Tony, grumbling prettily at the awful coffee she had had to drink at Colonel Howes'. 'Darling,' she begged Leonora, 'do make me a cup—you make such good coffee.'

She settled down in her chair and turned to Tony. 'Now, tell me all the latest gossip...'

Her father wasn't best pleased to learn that Tony had come for the weekend. He loved his daughter dearly, was aware that she was missing the kind of life a girl of her age should be enjoying but was not sure what to do about it. When Tony had swept her off her feet and he had seen the happiness in her face, he had been glad for her sake, although he had had to bury the vague dislike he had for him. If Leonora loved him and he would make her happy, then that was more important than his own feelings. Tony, after all, was a successful young man, able to give Leonora the comforts and small luxuries which he, her father, had been unable to afford.

He expressed a pleasure he didn't feel and told her he would be down to lunch and she whisked herself away to finish the beds and tidy first the rooms and then herself. There wasn't time to change into something more eye-catching than the sweater and skirt but at least she could do something to her face and hair.

Going downstairs a little later, she could hear her mother and Tony laughing and talking in the drawing room, which gave her the chance to go to the kitchen and see what Nanny had found for lunch.

Cheese omelettes, they decided, and there was a tin of mushroom and garlic soup which they could eke out with some chicken stock. Melba toast and a salad.

'We'll worry about dinner presently,' promised Leonora. 'I'll do the table in a minute and after lunch I'll go down to the village. It had better be a joint, I suppose—five of us—roast this evening, cold tomorrow.'

That would make a hole in the housekeeping, she reflected, going to sit in the drawing room and listen to Tony being amusing about his life in London.

A good-looking man, she reflected lovingly, and such fun to be with. She hoped that once they were married she would make him happy—live his kind of life, like his friends, enjoy the dinner parties and theatres and social occasions which he had assured her were so very important to his work.

Presently she slipped away to see to lunch and give Nanny a hand, half hoping that he would go with her. But he merely smiled and waved a hand.

'Don't be too long, darling; I miss you.'

Perhaps it was as well that he had stayed talking to

her mother and father, she decided, beating eggs, making a salad, laying the table...

After lunch she told him that she was going to the village. He frowned for a moment then smiled. 'A chance for us to talk,' he told her. 'Not paying visits, I hope.'

'No, no, just some shopping. It'll give you an appetite for tea.'

They met the vicar in the village street and she left them talking while she bought the meat. They were still talking when she joined them again.

Tony put an arm around her shoulders. 'Do we know when we want to get married, darling?' he asked. 'It all depends, actually, but it won't be long now. A June wedding, perhaps. That is, if the bride agrees to that.'

The vicar looked pleased. 'We haven't had a wedding for some time,' he observed, 'and June is a delightful month in which to be married.'

'A nice old man,' said Tony as they started back home. 'Very keen to see us married, isn't he?'

'Did you mean that—June—you said...?'

He took her free hand in his. 'Why not, darling? It will be a bit of a rush—but I suppose we could get the place tidied up by then.'

'What place?'

He stopped and turned to look at her. 'Leonora, surely you can see for yourself that that great house is too much for your father and mother? Suppose we move them out to something smaller? There's a nice little property a couple of miles away on the road to Bath. I'll have the house completely refurbished and it'll be a marvellous headquarters for me—us. Weekends for clients and friends. We'll have a flat in town, of course, but it's an easy run. I might even give you a car of your own so that you can go to and fro whenever you want.'

Leonora stared at him. 'You don't mean any of that, do you? I mean, turning Mother and Father out of their home? It's been in the family for almost two hundred years; Father would die; it's—it's his blood. Mother has all her friends here and she loves the house too—she came here when she married Father. It's a joke, isn't it?'

He put his arm round her shoulders. 'Darling, it's not a joke, it's common sense—can't you see that? Your father isn't exactly in the best of health, is he? Supposing he were to die—what would your mother do? Try and run this place on her own? She hasn't the faintest idea how to do it...'

'You forget me.' Leonora had twisted away from him. 'It's my home too and I won't leave it. And Father's almost well again—you heard what Dr Galbraith said—'

'A country GP?' Tony sounded derisive. 'He'll say whatever he thinks his patients want to hear.'

'That isn't true. What an abominable thing to say.' She began to walk on and he caught up with her and took her arm.

'Darling, I'm sorry if I've made you cross. All right, I won't say another word about your parents leaving home, but you must know that your father is in financial difficulties, and what will happen if they foreclose the mortgage?'

That brought her up short. 'Mortgage? I didn't know...'

'How do you suppose he's been able to stay here for so long?'

'How did you know?'

'I make it my business to know these things. Besides, I am concerned for you, Leonora.'

'Oh.' She felt guilty then for suspecting him. Suspecting him of what? she wondered. 'I'm sorry, Tony. Don't let's talk about it any more. Father will get things sorted out once he is feeling quite well. Do please believe me when I say that nothing on earth will make Father or Mother move from the house, and that goes for me too!'

He caught her arm again. 'Darling, you're going to marry me, remember?' He laughed a gentle laugh which made her smile and then laugh with him.

They went on their way and just as they reached the open gates to the house Dr Galbraith drove past. He raised a hand in salute, wondering why the sight of Leonora apparently so happy in Tony's company should disturb him.

Probably because I don't like the fellow, he decided, and forgot about them.

The weekend went too quickly for Leonora. Of course, having Tony there made a lot of extra work; he had admitted soon after they'd met that he was quite useless around the house and since there was no need for him to do anything for himself at his flat—a service flat where he could get his meals and a cleaner came each day—he made no effort to help. Not that Leonora expected him to make his bed or wash up, but it would have been nice if he hadn't given Nanny his shoes to clean and expected his trousers pressed—or even if he'd carried a tray out to the kitchen...

It would be better when they were married, reflected Leonora; she was sure that he would be only too willing to help out when necessary once he realised that help was needed.

He went back very early on Monday morning, which meant that Leonora got up and cooked his breakfast first.

It also meant that he used up almost all the hot water from the boiler and woke everyone up.

'I'll be down again just as soon as I can spare the time,' he told Leonora. 'And when I come do be ready for me, darling, and we'll have an evening out. Bath, perhaps? A decent meal and we could dance after.'

She agreed happily, ignoring the bit about the decent meal. Sunday lunch had been excellent, she had thought—roast beef, Yorkshire pudding, baked potatoes, vegetables from the garden and an apple tart for pudding. That was surely a decent meal? She kissed him goodbye and begged him to phone when he had time. 'Or write.'

'Write? My dear girl, when do I ever have time to write letters?' He squeezed her arm and gave her a charming smile. 'Be good.'

She gravely said, 'Yes, Tony,' and he laughed as he got into the car.

'Not much chance of being anything else, is there?' he shouted at her as he started the engine.

He would have to go carefully, he decided as he drove; no more mention of moving her mother and father out of the house. Perhaps it might be a good idea to wait until they were married. He had no doubt at all that he could persuade her to do anything he asked of her once she was his wife.

A few weeks of comfortable living, new clothes, new faces, meals out—once she had a taste of all the things a girl wanted in the way of a carefree life she would come round to his way of thinking. The more he saw of the house, the more he intended to have it...

Leonora, happily unaware of his schemes, went in-doors, placated her parents with very early morning tea, soothed a grumpy Nanny and went up to the attics to see if the rain had come in during the night. It had.

# CHAPTER THREE

AT ABOUT the same time as Tony was getting into his car to drive back to London, Dr Galbraith was letting himself into his house. He had been called out in the very early hours to a farm some miles away from the village where the farmer's elderly father had suffered a stroke and he'd waited with him until the ambulance had come to take him to Bath. He had followed it to the hospital, made sure that his patient was in good hands and then driven himself back home.

There was no question of going back to bed; he had morning surgery and a scattered round before mothers and babies' clinic in the early afternoon. He went quietly across the square hall and up the uncarpeted oak staircase to his room at the front of the old house. He had his hand on the door when another door at the far end of the passage opened and a tall, bony man emerged.

He was middle-aged, with a long, narrow face, dark hair streaked with grey, combed carefully over a bald patch, and an expression of gloom.

'Good morning, sir. You'll need a cup of coffee. I'll bring it up at once. Breakfast in an hour suit you?'

'Admirably, Cricket. I'm famished.'

Cricket went back to his room, shaking his head in a disapproving manner. He never failed to disapprove when the doctor was called out at night, but that didn't prevent him from making sure that there was a hot drink and a meal waiting for him. He had been with the doctor for a number of years now, running his house to perfection, cooking delicious meals, making sure that the cleaning lady did her work properly. In fact, he was a treasure.

The doctor drank his coffee, showered, dressed and went downstairs to his breakfast. It was light now, a chilly, breezy March morning, and he opened the door to the garden before going into the small sitting room at the back of the house, where Cricket had laid his breakfast.

It was a charming room, facing the rising sun, furnished comfortably with some nice old pieces and decidedly cosy, unlike the drawing room which was rather grand with its magnificent carpet, vast bow-fronted cabinets and the pair of sofas, one at each side of the marble fireplace. The drawing room also had comfortable chairs arranged here and there and a beautiful drum table in the bay window overlooking the front garden. It was a room the doctor used seldom, for dinner parties and on the occasions when his friends came to stay.

There was a dining room too, on the opposite side of the hall, with its Regency mahogany table and chairs and the splendid sideboard, and at the back of the hall his study, the room he used most of all.

It was a large house for an unmarried man but he was a big man and needed space around him. Besides, he loved the old place, having first seen it some years earlier when he had come to visit Dr Fleming, whom he had known for some time. It had seemed an act of Providence when he had agreed to take over Dr Fleming's practice and Buntings had been on the market.

He had his surgery in the village—a cottage which had been converted into a consulting room and a waiting room—although he saw patients at his home if necessary.

This morning there were more patients than usual: neglected colds which had settled on chests, elderly people with arthritis and rheumatism, a broken arm, a sprained ankle, septic fingers. Nothing dramatic, but they kept him busy for most of the morning; he was late starting his round.

He was barely a mile out of the village when his car phone rang. Mrs Crisp, his part-time receptionist and secretary, sounded urgent.

'There's a call from Willer's Farm. Mrs Willer—she's on her own except for a farm lad. The tractor driver has had an accident—a bad one, she says. Mr Willer's away—gone to a cattle market. She phoned Beckett's Farm but couldn't get an answer. There's no one else nearby.'

'Tell her I'm on my way. I should be there in twenty minutes.'

He put his large foot down and sent the car speeding along the road and then braked hard to avoid Leonora with Wilkins, coming round the curve in the middle of the road.

She nipped to one side, dragging Wilkins with her, and shouted sorry and would have gone on. He had come to a halt, though, and had the car door open, so that she felt compelled to repeat her apologies.

'Never mind that,' said the doctor impatiently. 'You're just what I need. You know Willer's Farm. There's been an accident there. I'm on my way and it seems there's no one there except Mrs Willer and a lad. I shall need help. Jump in, will you? I could use another pair of hands.'

'Wilkins?'

'In the car.' He leaned over and opened the door and

Wilkins got in without being asked; a lazy dog by nature, he thought the chance of a ride wasn't to be missed.

Leonora got in beside the doctor, remarking calmly, 'I don't know anything about first aid, or at least not much, but I'm strong. I was going to the shop for Nanny; would you mind if I phoned her? She's waiting for some braising steak.'

The doctor handed her the phone without speaking and listened to her quiet voice telling Nanny that she might be home rather later than expected and perhaps someone else could go to the village. 'I've got Wilkins with me and we'll be back when you see us.'

She replaced the phone and sat quietly as he drove through the narrow, high-hedged lanes, wondering what they would find when they got to the farm.

Mrs Willer came running out to meet them as the doctor slowed the car across the farmyard, which was rutted and muddy and redolent of farmyard smells.

'He's on Lower Pike. The boy's with him; I came down to show you the way. He's real bad. It's 'is foot—got it caught in the tractor as 'e fell out.'

The doctor was bending over the car's boot, handing things to Leonora. He said merely, 'We'll take a look. How long has he been lying there? Is he conscious?'

'Now 'e is, Doctor... Not at first, 'e wasn't. Banged 'is 'ead.'

They were crossing the yard now, making for the open fields beyond, which sloped gently uphill to Higher Pike, and going at a good pace. Leonora, a splendid walker, found herself making an effort to keep up with the doctor's strides.

The next twenty minutes were like a very unpleasant dream. The tractor had reared up and toppled backwards and although Ben, the driver, had been flung free his foot had been trapped by the superstructure.

The doctor got down beside him and opened his bag. 'Pain bad?' he asked, and when Ben nodded he filled a syringe and plunged its contents into the arm he had bared. Presently, as the dope took effect, he examined his patient and then bent over his foot, trapped by a heavy iron crossbar.

'Open that bag,' He nodded towards the zippered bag he had been carrying. 'Hand me the things from it as I ask for them.' He looked over his shoulder. 'And you, boy, fetch me a spade, two spades, anything to dig with.'

He busied himself cleaning and covering the crushed foot, and Leonora, very much on her mettle, handed things from the bag when he asked for them. Most of them she had never seen before—forceps and probes and some nasty-looking scissors. Most of the time she managed not to look too closely…

All the while he worked, the doctor talked to Ben— a soothing flow of words uttered in a quiet, reassuring voice. 'We're going to dig the earth from under your foot to relieve the pressure on it,' he explained. 'I'm going to phone for an ambulance and help now; you'll soon be comfortable.'

Leonora listened to him talking into his phone; it seemed hours since they had arrived but when she glanced at her watch she saw that it was barely fifteen minutes.

The boy came back then with the spades. Dr Galbraith took one, handed him the other and told him what they were going to do, then he said to Leonora, 'Come here and kneel by Ben's foot. Don't touch it yet, but be ready to steady it.'

She knelt gingerly. The tractor loomed huge above her

and she tried not to think what would happen should it shift. The foot was swathed in a protective covering, bloodstained but not frighteningly so. She crept nearer and held her hands ready.

They dug cautiously, inch by inch, so that presently there was a bit of space between Ben's foot and the crossbar. It would need far more room than that to free the foot, she thought; the tractor would have to be righted.

The digging stopped then and the doctor took her place, his arm sheltering the foot as far as possible. If the tractor moves…thought Leonora, and didn't dare think further.

'Take Mrs Willer to the house and help her pack a bag for Ben,' said the doctor. 'Everything he'll need at the hospital. And then come back here.'

She led a shocked Mrs Willer back to the house, found a bag and together they packed it. They had done that when they heard the high-pitched wail of the ambulance and the louder, deeper note of the fire engine, and by the time they had got back to the tractor there were men everywhere.

It took time to right the tractor and more time to inspect Ben's foot thoroughly. Finally he was on a stretcher, being carried to the ambulance.

In answer to his, 'Come along, Leonora,' she followed the doctor to the car and got in. Wilkins, snoozing on the back seat, opened an eye in greeting and went back to sleep and she sat watching the doctor as he spoke to Mrs Willer.

Getting in beside her, he said, 'You have been a great help; thank you, Leonora. Ben is going to the Royal National at Bath; I must go there and speak to the casualty officer.' He picked up the phone. 'I'll explain to Nanny…' Which he did before handing the phone to her.

Nanny sounded anxious. 'Miss Leonora, are you all right? Am I to tell your ma and pa?'

'I'm fine, Nanny, really I am. I shan't be home for a little while. If you tell them that without any details…'

'Anyway, you're safe enough with Dr Galbraith and you've got the phone.'

At the hospital she got out with Wilkins and walked round with him while the doctor went inside. She was hungry and untidy and her skirt was covered with dried earth from the ploughed field but she felt happy; she had made herself useful even in a humble capacity and Dr Galbraith's brisk thanks had warmed her. Presently she saw him leave the hospital and went back to the car, into which Wilkins scrambled with evident relief. He had walked enough.

'Ben—that foot?' said Leonora, getting into the car. 'Will he be all right?'

'He's in Theatre now. If anyone can save it, it's the man who's operating.'

'Oh, good.' She added fiercely, 'He needs his feet— it's his livelihood…'

When he didn't answer, she said, 'What about your other patients? You had just started your round, hadn't you?'

'Mrs Crisp has sorted them out for me; there's nothing really urgent. I've a surgery this evening and I can do a round this afternoon. We'll go back now and clean up and have a meal.'

He picked up the phone again. 'Cricket? I'm bringing Miss Crosby back with me for lunch. We'll need to clean up first—say half an hour? Something quick.'

'Who's Cricket?' asked Leonora. 'And you don't have

to ask me to lunch. Drop me off at the gate as you go past.'

'Cricket is my manservant; he runs my home. I should be totally lost without him. And will you lunch with me, Leonora? It is the least I can do to make amends for spoiling your quiet day.' He glanced at her. 'Besides, you're badly in need of a wash and brush-up.'

It was hardly a flattering reason for being asked to lunch. She had half a mind to refuse but curiosity to see his house and find out something about him got the better of her resentment, and then common sense came to the rescue and she laughed. He was offering practical help and she was hungry and, as he had pointed out, badly in need of a good wash.

'Thank you; that would be nice,' she told him sedately.

It was as he drew up before his door that Leonora spoke again.

'What about Wilkins? Do you have a dog?'

He came round the car to open her door. 'He's welcome to come in. I have a dog. My sister has borrowed him for a week or two while her husband is away. He'll be back next week. Cricket has two cats. I hardly think they will be in any danger from Wilkins; a remarkably mild animal, isn't he?'

'He's a darling,' said Leonora warmly, 'and he's partial to cats.'

Cricket opened the door, shook the hand she offered and instantly approved of her. Even with a smudge on her cheek and dirty hands she was a very pretty girl. Plenty of her, too; he liked a woman to look like a woman and here was one who, he decided, lived up to his strict ideals of what a young lady should be.

He ushered her indoors, tut-tutted gently at the state

of her skirt and led her to the downstairs cloakroom. Halfway across the hall the doctor called after them.

'Get Miss Crosby a dressing gown, Cricket, and see if you can get some of that mud off her skirt, will you?'

'Certainly, sir. Is ten minutes too soon for lunch?'

'Just right. If I'm not down show Miss Crosby into the sitting room, will you? Thanks!'

Then he went up upstairs two at a time and Cricket ushered Leonora into the cloakroom, begged a moment's grace and came back within a minute with a bathrobe. 'If you would let me have your skirt, Miss Crosby, I'll have it as good as new before you leave.' He smiled at her. 'I will keep an eye on your dog, miss.'

She thanked him and, left alone, began on the task of getting clean again. Her skirt was horribly stained and it smelled, naturally enough, of the farm.

Presently, with a nicely washed face and her hair neatly pinned up, she got into the robe, opened the door cautiously and peered round it. Cricket had said that he would show her where to go...

Dr Galbraith was in the hall, lounging against the wall, Wilkins panting happily beside him.

'Come on out,' he invited. 'Cricket has lunch ready and I have to be at the surgery in less than an hour.'

He sounded, reflected Leonora, like someone's brother, and she did as she was told, following him, a little hampered by the robe, across the hall and into the sitting room overlooking the garden. Their lunch had been laid on a round table near the open fire and something smelled delicious. She pushed the over-long sleeves up her arms and sat down without further ado to sample Cricket's artichoke soup.

The doctor had made no comment about her appearance but he smiled a little at the sensible way she had tucked up the sleeves and wrapped the yards of extra material around her person, and he liked her lack of self-consciousness.

The soup was followed by a cheese pudding and a salad and they drank tonic water before Cricket brought in the coffee-tray. Since there wasn't much time and it was obvious to her that this wasn't a social occasion, Leonora made no attempt to make conversation.

The moment they had drunk their coffee she said, 'I'll go and put my own clothes on again. You'll want to be going.' She smiled at him. 'Thank you for lunch; it was delicious.'

He got up with her. 'I'll be in the garden with Wilkins,' he told her, and watched her gather up the trailing robe as she crossed the hall. A sensible girl, he thought; no nonsense about her. Beamish was a lucky man. He frowned. She was too good for the fellow.

Cricket had worked wonders with the stains on her skirt. Really, they had almost gone; he had pressed it too. How wonderful to have someone like that to look after you, Leonora mused. No wonder the doctor wasn't married; he must be very comfortable as he was. She hurried into her clothes, thanked Cricket for his help and got into the car once more.

'Drop us off in the village,' she told the doctor. 'Anywhere along the main street will do.'

'I shall drive you home.' His voice dared her to argue about it and she sat silent for a moment, trying to think of something to say. At length she said, 'You told me you had a dog; what do you call him?'

'Tod.'

'Unusual—is it a foreign name?'

She saw his slow smile. 'No, no. It isn't a name of

my choosing but a young lady for whom I have an affection named him and Tod it is.'

Ha, thought Leonora, the girlfriend—there was bound to be someone. Her fertile imagination was already at work. Small and fragile and blue-eyed. Fair hair beautifully dressed, and wearing the very latest in fashion. She would have one of those sickening voices that made one squirm. Leonora, disliking this figment of her imagination, reflected that she would be the kind of girl to call a dog by such a silly name.

She said inadequately, 'How nice,' and waved to Mrs Pike standing outside her shop.

When he stopped before her home she said frostily, still influenced by her fancies, 'Thank you so much, Doctor. I do hope you won't be too busy for the rest of the day. And I hope that poor man will get better.'

He got out to open her door and stood beside her, looking at her thoughtfully. 'I'll let you know, and it is I who thank you for your help.'

He waited while she opened the door, and Wilkins rushed past her, intent on getting to the warmth of the kitchen. 'Well, goodbye,' said Leonora awkwardly, and went indoors.

Her mother and father were in the drawing room.

'Darling, where have you been? So awkward—I mean, Nanny had to leave everything and go down to the village. Why ever should Dr Galbraith want you? An accident at Willer's Farm, Nanny says. Surely they could have managed without you?'

Leonora opened her mouth to explain but her mother went on, 'Your Tony phoned. He was quite annoyed because you weren't here. Perhaps you had better give him a ring presently and explain.'

'Did he say why he had phoned?'

'No, dear. We were chatting for a while and I quite forgot to ask.'

Leonora went to the kitchen and found Nanny preparing oxtail for supper.

'I'm sorry, Nanny, but Dr Galbraith didn't give me a chance to refuse…'

'Quite right too. Bad accident, was it? He wouldn't have asked for your help if he hadn't needed it. Tell me about it. It's too early for tea but you could get the tray ready while I finish this and get it into the oven.'

So Leonora recited her morning's activities, not leaving anything out, detailing her lunch and the perfections of the doctor's house.

'Sounds nice,' said Nanny. 'And that man of his—was he nice?'

'Yes, very. He took my skirt and cleaned it. You've no idea how filthy it was—he pressed it too.'

'I'm sorry about Ben, but the doctor will see him right and the Willers will keep an eye on him—give him light work if he can't manage his usual jobs.'

Leonora ate a scone from the plate Nanny had just put on the table.

'You'll get fat,' said Nanny. 'Your young man rang up. Put out, he was.' She shot a quick glance at Leonora. 'Won't do no harm just for once…'

'What do you mean, Nanny?'

'Well, love, the men like to do a bit of chasing. It's not a bad idea to be difficult to get at times.'

'Nanny, you naughty old thing, where did you learn to play fast and loose with the gentlemen?' Leonora was laughing.

'Never you mind! It's sound common sense. No need to say you're sorry you weren't waiting here by the phone in the hopes he'd ring up.'

She picked up the plate of scones. 'They're for tea, Miss Leonora, and I'm not making another batch. You'd best go and tidy yourself. What the doctor thought of you I'll never know.'

The doctor was a man to keep his thoughts to himself so Nanny was never likely to find out. All the same she would have been pleased if she had found out; she had never taken a fancy to Tony Beamish—not good enough for her Miss Leonora, but clever enough to make her think she was in love with him.

'No good'll come of it!' said Nanny, buttering scones.

Leonora, feeling guilty but bearing Nanny's advice in mind, made no attempt to phone Tony, although once or twice during the rest of the afternoon and evening she very nearly did. She was on the point of going to bed when he rang up.

He was still annoyed. 'Where were you?' he wanted to know. 'What's all this about going to an accident and why didn't you phone me as soon as you got home?'

'Well, I am never quite sure where you are. It was a bad accident—one of the men on Willer's Farm—the tractor overturned—'

'Spare me the details,' begged Tony impatiently. 'And why you had to have anything to do with it I can't imagine.'

She told him, leaving out quite a bit because he was getting impatient again.

'Utterly ridiculous,' said Tony. 'That doctor must be thoroughly incompetent.'

'Don't be silly!' Leonora heard his indrawn breath. She had never called him silly before.

'I'm busy,' snapped Tony, 'and obviously you're overwrought. I hope you will have the good sense to keep out of the man's way in future.' He rang off without saying goodbye, confident that he would get a letter from her in the morning begging forgiveness for being such a bad-tempered girl.

Leonora, however, had no intention of putting pen to paper. Love was blind but not as blind as all that; Tony hadn't sounded like Tony at all. Was there a side to him which she hadn't yet discovered? It wasn't as though she particularly liked Dr Galbraith. For that matter, he didn't particularly like her, ordering her around and telling her what to do and that she needed a wash.

Despite the horror of the accident, she had enjoyed herself. Being useful—really useful—had made her feel quite different. She would drive to Bath and visit Ben. Perhaps there was something that her father could do for him—not financial help, of course, that wasn't possible, but influence with authority, perhaps.

She drove over to Bath two days later with a box of fruit and some flowers and found her way to the ward where Ben was lying.

He was in bed, propped up by pillows, his leg under a cradle, his weather-beaten face pale and lined, although he greeted her cheerfully.

She sat down beside his bed, offered the fruit and flowers and asked how he was getting on.

''Ad me foot put together again,' he told her. 'Take a bit of time, it will, but I'll be able to walk, so they tell me. Mustn't grumble.'

'How long will you be here?'

'A while yet. Got to learn to walk again, 'a'n't I?'

'Yes, of course. You'll go back to Willer's?'

'Mr Willer, 'e'll see me right…'

'I think you can claim compensation, Ben.'

'So 'tis said. Mr Willer, 'e'll attend to that.' He said awkwardly, 'I'm downright thankful for your help, Miss

Crosby. Dr Galbraith told me as 'ow you gived a hand. 'E's been a trump too. Comes to see me regular; knows the surgeon who done me foot.'

'That's nice. Ben, is there anything that you want? Money? Books? Clothes?'

'I'm fine, thank you, miss. Proper good treatment I'm getting too. Pretty nurses and all.'

She stayed for an hour, dredging up bits of local gossip to interest him, but when the tea-trolley arrived she bade him goodbye. 'I'll be back,' she told him. 'The Willers are coming to see you in a day or two—I'll come again next week.'

She left the ward and was walking along the long corridor which led to the main staircase when she saw Dr Galbraith coming towards her. He wasn't alone; there were a couple of younger men in white jackets and a white-coated man with him, and although he wasn't wearing a white coat Leonora had the feeling that he was as remote as his companion, the possessor of knowledge she knew nothing of and therefore someone difficult to get to know, to be friends with.

Face to face, she wished him a good afternoon and made to walk on, but he put out an arm and caught her gently by the wrist.

'Leonora? You have been to see Ben? This is Mr Kirby who operated on his foot.'

He looked at his companion. 'This is Miss Crosby, who very kindly came to my aid at the farm.'

She shook hands and murmured that she mustn't keep them.

'How did you come? I'll give you a lift back...'

'I drove over, but thank you all the same.' She included everyone in her goodbye, aware that she wasn't behaving in her usual calm and collected manner. The

look of amusement on Dr Galbraith's face sent the colour into her cheeks, which made things even worse.

It was two days later when her mother looked up from
her letters over breakfast.

'Our little dinner party, Leonora. I thought twelve of
us—just a nice number, don't you agree? We'll ask
Colonel Howes and Nora, the Willoughbys, of course,
the Merediths, the vicar—Dulcie Hunt is visiting her
mother so he'll be glad of a little social life—and Dr
Galbraith, and Tony simply must manage to come. We'll
have it on a Saturday; that should make it easy for him.'

She counted on her fingers. 'With us that's twelve—'

'Mother,' said Leonora, 'I don't think it's a good idea
to ask Dr Galbraith if Tony comes. They don't like each
other...'

'Nonsense, darling, of course they do.' She made a
great business of buttering her toast. 'Anyway, I've already invited them.' She gave Leonora a quick glance.
'Well, I hadn't much to do yesterday so I wrote the
invitations and your father gave them to the postman in
the afternoon.'

'When for?' asked Leonora. 'And have you any ideas
about feeding them?'

'Darling, what a funny way of putting it... Saturday
week. That gives Tony lots of time to arrange his work.
I thought we might have artichoke soup. You did say
there were a lot still in the garden. Willer sent over two
brace of pheasants—a kind of thank-you for your help,
he said; wasn't that nice? There must be some kind of
vegetables still in the kitchen garden to go with them,
and I'm sure Nanny will think of some delicious sweet.
Thank heaven there are at least a couple of bottles of
claret in the cellar.'

She smiled, well pleased with herself. 'So you see,

darling, there's almost nothing to do and it'll cost hardly anything, and if we use the best silver and those lace table mats and you concoct one of your centrepieces it will all look much more than it is, if you see what I mean.'

'Yes, Mother,' said Leonora. Of course it would cost something—the best coffee beans, cream, cranberries for the sauce, more cream for the soup, after-dinner mints, sherry—two bottles at least—and a bottle of whisky for any of the men who wanted it. Her father wouldn't take kindly to her using his...

Then there would be bacon and baby sausages to go with the pheasant, and the 'delicious sweet' still to be decided upon. They couldn't afford it but it was too late to tell her mother that. Leonora cleared up the breakfast things and went to the kitchen to give a hand with the washing-up and confer with Nanny about a suitable pudding.

Tony phoned during the week. He had managed to squeeze out a weekend, he told her, and would be down at teatime on the Saturday, adding the rider that he hoped her father would be up to a dinner party. 'He's not as young as he was!' he cautioned. 'We must keep an eye on him.'

He was in such good humour that she thought it prudent not to mention that Dr Galbraith was to be one of the guests. After all, there would be twelve of them there and they didn't need to do more than bid each other a civil good evening. She must remember to make sure that they were as far apart at the table as possible.

She went once more to see Ben, anxious not to meet the doctor in the hospital but disappointed nonetheless when she didn't. Ben was doing well. He had been out of bed on crutches and was having physiotherapy. It would take a bit of time, he assured her, but he'd be as good as new by the time they'd finished with him.

She left him a bag of fruit and some magazines and drove home. When she saw Dr Galbraith again she must ask him just how fit Ben would be. The thought struck her that she might not have the chance to speak to him at the dinner party, not if Tony was there…

Saturday week came and with it a dozen or more things to see to. The floral arrangement she had already contrived from various bits of greenery, some daffodils and primroses and aconites from the neglected border at the front of the house. She polished the table, helped Nanny put in the extra leaf and arranged the lace mats.

The silver was old, kept in a baize bag in what had once been the butler's pantry, and she had polished it to a dazzling gleam; she had done the same with the crystal glasses and had washed the Coalport dinner service. They combined to make an elegant dinner table, and her mother, coming to see that things were just as she liked them, gave a satisfied sigh.

'We may be poor,' she observed, 'but we can still show the world a brave face. It looks very nice, dear.'

Leonora filled the Georgian salt cellars and went to the kitchen to start the syllabub. A dozen eggs was an extravagance; on the other hand the yolks could be made into *créme brûlée*, which if it wasn't all eaten at dinner could be used up on the following day…

She went upstairs after tea and looked through her wardrobe. Her clothes were good, for they had been bought when there had been enough money to have the best. They still looked good, too, but were sadly out of date. There was a silver-grey velvet somewhere at the back of the cupboard…

She hauled it out and tried it on and it didn't look too

bad—very plain, with its modest, unfashionable neckline and long sleeves, but it fitted her nicely. She had a quick shower and got dressed; Tony had said that he would arrive in plenty of time for drinks and there were still one or two jobs to do in the kitchen, where Nanny was working miracles with the pheasants.

Downstairs she put on a pinny, tucked up her sleeves and began to whip the cream. The evening should be a success, she thought; her mother was pleased, her father was better, though somewhat irascible, Tony was coming...

He had come; he stood in the doorway looking at her. Frowning. She looked up, smiling as he came in and then puzzled.

'My dear girl, do you have to spend your time in the kitchen? The guests will be here in ten minutes or so and I expected to be met by an elegant fiancée sitting in the drawing room doing nothing.'

She made the mistake of thinking that he was joking. 'Tony, don't be so absurd. Of course I have to be here. Nanny can't possibly manage on her own; she's doing two people's work as it is. I'm almost ready. Go and pour yourself a drink; Father and Mother should be down at any minute.'

He turned away without another word, and since the cream had reached the peak of perfection she hardly noticed his going. The fleeting thought that he hadn't kissed her or even said how glad he was to see her passed through her head, but just at that moment she had a lot to think about if the dinner party was to be a success.

Ten minutes later she slipped into the drawing room to find that everyone had arrived, and she went from one to the other, exchanging greetings. They were all old friends—excepting Dr Galbraith, elegant in black tie, talking to Nora. He smiled down at her and she offered a hand, and since Tony had made no effort to speak to her, had barely glanced in her direction she let it lie in his firm grasp for longer than necessary and gave him a bewitching smile in return.

'I'm glad you could come. Have you got your dog—Tod—home yet?'

'Yesterday. He brought my sister with him. She had to return home at once, though—her youngest has the measles.'

'Oh, what bad luck, but nice to get it over with when you're young. We had it at about the same time, didn't we, Nora? We must have been seven or eight...'

The doctor stared down at her; she must have been an engaging small girl with those enormous eyes, he thought.

'Yes, well,' said Leonora, aware of the stare. 'I must just nip along to the kitchen—the soup, you know...'

They watched her go. 'She's such a dear,' said Nora. 'She practically runs this great place on her own. If it wasn't for Nanny she could never cope.'

Mrs Sims from the village, who occasionally obliged with the heavy cleaning, was waiting in the kitchen ready to carry in the soup tureen; the pheasants were done to a turn, everything was fine, declared Nanny.

Leonora went back to the drawing room, bent to whisper to her mother and everyone crossed the hall to the dining room. Leonora had had a fire burning in its elegant grate all day, sighing over every shovelful of coal and every log, but appearances had to be kept up and the room was nicely warm now. She took her seat beside Tony and watched Mrs Sims place the tureen in front of her mother. So far, so good...

# CHAPTER FOUR

THERE was a good deal of lively conversation over the soup. Leonora, listening to Colonel Howes describing the delights of a genuine Indian curry, hardly noticed Tony's silence on her other side. When she was free to turn to him, he was talking to Nora beside him.

She glanced down the table; Dr Galbraith was sitting beside her mother, who was talking animatedly, and the vicar and her father were discussing the local fishing.

The soup plates were removed and her father began to carve the pheasants—quite a lengthy business, but the claret had loosened tongues and everyone was chatting, relaxed among friends...

'Will you stay until Monday?' she asked Tony. She smiled at him, no longer vexed; he was probably tired after a busy week and he hated to see her working around the house.

'There doesn't seem to be much point if you're going to be in the kitchen all day.'

She refused to get needled. 'Well, I shan't be. We might go for a good walk—blow the London cobwebs away.'

'London at this time of year is rather delightful. How is your father? I thought he looked very tired.'

'Did you?' She frowned. 'He's so much better—'

'I shall have a word with that doctor of his before I go—make sure he's getting proper treatment.'

Leonora helped herself to sprouts. 'Quite unnecessary, Tony; Father is in good hands.'

'It seems to me that that fellow has cast a spell over you all—he's probably quite incompetent!'

Leonora's eyes glittered with temper. 'That's an abominable thing to say. Would you have known how to get a man with a crushed foot free from a farm tractor?'

She turned back to Colonel Howes and began an animated conversation about the extension to be built to the village hall, and the doctor, watching her from under lowered lids and replying suitably to Lady Crosby's chatter, wondered what she and Tony were quarrelling about. They were being very discreet about it, but they were quarrelling.

In due course the pheasant was replaced by syllabub and the *crème brûlée,* and since Lady Crosby refused to accede to modern ideas the ladies were led away to the drawing room while the men remained to drink the port Sir William had brought up from the cellar.

Leonora slid away as the ladies went into the drawing room, to reappear presently with the tray of coffee-pot, cream and sugar. The small table had already been placed by her mother's chair, bearing the Worcester coffee-cups and the silver dishes of after-dinner mints. By the time the men joined them, they were deep in comfortable talk—clothes, the price of food, their grandchildren, and the difficulty of getting a gardener.

When the men came in there was a good deal of rearranging of seats and Leonora was kept busy offering more coffee and refilling cups, and by the time she had seen to everyone Tony was sitting between Nora and Mrs Willoughby on one of the old-fashioned sofas. So she went and sat by the vicar and listened to him talking about his wife, to discover after a few minutes that Dr

Galbraith had joined them. A moment later her father walked over.

'Come along to my study,' he invited the vicar. 'I'll show you that new trout fly I've just tied.' Which left Leonora and the doctor together.

'A pleasant evening, Leonora.'

'Thank you.'

'Why were you and young Beamish quarrelling?' He smiled. 'Still are?'

She was getting used to the way he eschewed the soft approach. 'Well, you see, I was in the kitchen when he got here—and he was disappointed because I wasn't in the drawing room.'

'Quite.'

'I should have thought of that but I had the cream to whip. I didn't think it mattered much. I mean, would you have minded?'

'In the circumstances, and seeing that the success of the dinner party largely rested on the cream being properly whipped, no!' He put down his coffee-cup. 'But there was something else, wasn't there?'

'Well, yes. He thinks Father doesn't look well.' She went pink. 'He—he wondered if...'

'Ah—he doubts my expertise.'

'I'm so sorry. I mean, no one else does; we all trust you and think you're a very good doctor.'

He hid a smile. 'Thank you. I won't let it worry me.'

'He said that he would talk to you.'

'Splendid. And since he is coming to join us now, what could be a better opportunity?' He glanced at her troubled face. 'Go and talk to someone else,' he suggested quietly, and turned a bland face to Tony.

He stood up as Leonora moved away and Tony

frowned, put at a disadvantage by the doctor's height and size.

'You wanted to talk to me?' the doctor enquired pleasantly.

'Look here,' began Tony, 'I'm not at all happy about Sir William…'

Dr Galbraith said nothing.

'He isn't a young man.'

The doctor inclined his head; he looked so exactly like an eminent doctor listening with courteous patience to one of his patients that Tony's face darkened with annoyance.

'Isn't it ridiculous that Sir William should go on living in this great house? He needs to be in something smaller and modern where he would be properly looked after.' He caught the doctor's eye. 'Oh, Leonora looks after him very well, I know, but she's limited—no money. Now, if he were to sell the place or hand it over to her, I could restore it.'

'Yes?' queried the doctor gently. 'Would you live in it—with Leonora, of course?'

Tony said rudely, 'Oh, of course. We'd have a flat in town but we could come for weekends, bring guests.' He stopped, aware that he was talking too much. He essayed a smile. 'My dear chap, I'm sure you could persuade Sir William to settle in something more suitable to his age and lifestyle.'

The doctor said evenly, 'No, I couldn't do that. It isn't my business. Sir William lives here, it is his home, his ancestor's home, he loves it. Surely if you intend to restore the place there is no reason why he and Lady Crosby shouldn't live here? Why move? There is ample room for them, is there not?'

'I can't see that it is any concern of yours,' said Tony sulkily.

The vicar had joined them again and presently Tony went away. The talk hadn't been very successful, he reflected, and went in search of Leonora. He found her talking to Nora, who finally drifted away, so that he was able to give her his version of his talk with Dr Galbraith.

'Well,' said Leonora in a matter-of-fact way, 'he's quite right; there's no reason why Father should move from here. It's a silly idea. It would break his heart, besides being an enormous undertaking. You have no idea of the stuff that's stored in the attics.'

She saw his annoyance and said quickly, 'It's very good of you to bother, Tony—I'm sure Father appreciates your concern; we all do.' She added soberly, 'I suppose in due time I shall inherit the place, but not for a long while yet. If you want to restore it then, I won't mind...'

Tony said soberly, 'My dear girl, we shall probably be in our dotage. The place needs a complete overhaul now but it can't be done while your mother and father are still here.'

Leonora gave him a puzzled look and he saw that he had said too much. He took her arm and smiled at her. 'Darling, don't let's worry about it. As you say, your parents are very happy here. It is a lovely old place, just the right background for a dinner party. I must say it's a splendid evening and dinner was delicious. I can see that I am going to be very proud of my wife.'

They were words which dulled the faint feeling of unease Leonora had been trying to ignore. She told him about the pheasants and the artichoke soup. 'So, you see, it cost hardly anything...'

He squeezed her arm and laughed with her and Dr

Galbraith, watching them from the other side of the room, thought it was a great pity that a sensible girl like Leonora should be taken in by young Beamish. She was too good for him and too honest, and once she had married him and found out about him, as she was bound to do eventually, she would keep her marriage vows and be a loyal wife and quietly break her heart. A pity that some decent man couldn't come along and marry her before Beamish had a chance to complete his plans.

It seemed strange to the doctor that Sir William hadn't seen what was happening, with all this talk about his health and the need to move away from his home. Could he not see that Beamish wanted to get his hands on the lovely old place and use it for his own ends? The doctor frowned; it seemed likely that the man was going to marry Leonora for that very reason.

He shrugged his enormous shoulders; it was none of his business.

Cricket, advancing to meet him as he let himself into his house later that evening, enquired as to whether he had had an enjoyable time. 'A very pleasant young lady, Miss Crosby,' said Cricket. 'I have had occasion to have a few words with Miss South—her old nanny, sir—and she told me that she is a most capable person and shortly to be married.'

'You old gossip,' said the doctor cheerfully. 'I had a very pleasant evening and now I am going to take Tod for a quick walk. I'll lock up when I get back.'

Presently he did just that, saw Tod into his basket in the kitchen and took himself off to bed. He had had a long and busy day and he slept the sleep of a tired man, never once thinking of Leonora.

However, Leonora, tired though she was, didn't sleep well. Tony had sewn the seeds of doubt in her mind;

perhaps her father would be better off living in a smaller house where there was no need of buckets to catch the drips when it rained and the plumbing was up to date. What did Tony intend to do with her house after they were married? He had been enthusiastic about restoring it but for what reason? He had made it plain on several occasions that they would live in London because of his work.

She shook up her pillows and tried to settle down. They would have to have a talk about it, fix the date of the wedding and discuss their future. She closed her eyes and presently slept uneasily.

There was no chance to talk to Tony in the morning; when they got back from church he went with her father to the library and over lunch the talk was of nothing much. She suggested over their coffee that they might go for a walk but he told her that he would have to go back to London within the hour. 'You should see the pile of work on my desk,' he told her. 'But I was determined to come to your dinner party, darling. It was a great success. I'll be down again just as soon as I can manage it.'

She said soberly, 'Tony, I think we must have a talk—about the wedding and where we're to live and—oh, a whole lot of things I'm not sure about.'

'Of course, darling. We will the very next time I come.' He bent to kiss her. 'You're my darling girl and we are going to be very happy.' He spoilt it for her by adding, 'And very rich...'

'I don't care about being rich, Tony.'

'You will. Lovely clothes, and theatres, and meeting all the right people.'

She said coolly, 'The right people live here too, Tony!'

He kissed her again. 'Yes, of course they do. I'll phone you this evening.'

It was later in the week, when she had walked down to the village to Mrs Pike's shop, that that lady leaned over the counter to say confidentially, 'Those gentlemen staying over at the Blue Man—they've not been bothering you, Miss Leonora?'

'Bothering me? I didn't know there was anyone staying in the village, Mrs Pike, and why should they bother me?'

'Well, they been asking questions about the house, wanting to know how many rooms there was and how much land there was with it. When Mr Bowles over at the Blue Man spoke up and asked them why they didn't go to the house and ask Sir William since they were so anxious to know, they shut up like clams, said as how they were just curious. All the same, they've been sitting in the bar of a night, dropping questions here and there. Your pa's not thinking of selling, like?'

'Absolutely not, Mrs Pike. What sort of men are they?'

'Oh, gents, miss, quite the city men, if you get my meaning; they wears ties and carries umbrellas. Nicely spoken too.'

'You don't know where they're from? I mean, has some house agent got it into his head that my father is going to sell the house? I can't understand it. Perhaps I'd better go across and tell them that they are mistaken.'

'Oh, I wouldn't do that, miss,' said Mrs Pike, 'seeing as how they'd know at once who you was. You leave it to me; I'll get my George to go over for a pint this evening. He's a sharp one; perhaps he can ferret something out.'

'Would he? That would be very kind. Mrs Pike, you

won't talk about this to anyone, will you? I can assure you that my father has absolutely no intention of leaving the house.' She picked up her shopping. 'I'll come down in the morning…'

She went back home wishing there were someone she could talk to about it, but that wasn't possible; her parents would be upset and worried and Nanny would probably go down to the Blue Man and demand to see these men and give them a piece of her mind. A pity that she wasn't on better terms with Dr Galbraith, she reflected; he was someone one could confide in and get sensible advice from in return.

She worried about it all day and half the night and, making some excuse about fetching a particular brand of biscuits Mrs Pike was getting for her, went to the village directly after breakfast.

There were several people in the shop, and when it was empty at last Mrs Pike seemed very reluctant to talk.

'Mr Pike heard something?' she asked Mrs Pike. 'Something you don't like to tell me?'

'Well, yes, miss. Mind you, it's only gossip; you can't believe half you hear these days. I dare say there's a good reason…'

Leonora smiled and looked so calm that Mrs Pike decided to talk after all.

'Well, it's like this, miss—these gentlemen has come here to look over the house and see if it's worth doing up and if the land is good for selling to build on…'

At Leonora's quick breath she paused. 'The house is to be a kind of headquarters for visiting businessmen— them big nobs with millions.' She eyed Leonora carefully. 'I hates to say this, Miss Crosby, but the man who sent them is your Mr Beamish.'

Leonora had gone very pale but she said composedly,

'Mrs Pike, I can't thank you enough—or Mr Pike—for your help. I'm sure there's some misunderstanding but at least I know whom to see about it. I'm quite sure that my father knows nothing about this but I'll talk to Mr Beamish about it. There must be an explanation.'

'Yes, miss, that's what we thought. Mr Beamish seems such a nice gentleman…'

'Yes,' said Leonora, and added, 'I'll be off. I want to do some gardening.'

She made herself walk normally out of the shop, even turning to smile at Mrs Pike from the doorway, and somehow she had to go through the village looking the same as usual. If she could manage not to think about it until she got home… She gulped; when she got home she wouldn't be able to think about it either, let alone say anything.

She marched down the street, saying good morning and smiling as she went, with Wilkins close at her heels. She was going past the surgery when Dr Galbraith came out, shutting the door behind him. She would have gone past him with a brief greeting but he fell into step beside her.

'What is the matter?' he asked, and added, 'No, don't tell me for the moment. The car's across the street; we'll go back to Buntings.'

Because she would have burst into tears if she had attempted to speak just then, she went with him and got into the car and sat silently with Wilkins' elderly whiskers pressed into the back of her neck.

At the house the doctor got out, opened her door, let Wilkins out, and as Cricket came to the door said briskly, 'Could we have coffee, Cricket? In the sitting room, I think; Wilkins can go into the garden with Tod.'

Cricket cast a look at Leonora's face, murmured

soothingly and went to the kitchen while the doctor led her across the hall and into the pleasant little room bright with sunshine.

The door to the garden was open and racing across the grass lawn came a dog, barking his pleasure at the sight of them. It was impossible to tell what kind of a dog he was, but there was a strong bias towards an Alsatian and more than a hint of retriever; he had a noble head and a curly coat and a feathery tail and liquid brown eyes.

'Tod,' said the doctor briefly. 'Sit down here; Wilkins can go into the garden too and make friends.' He said over one shoulder, 'Cry if you want to.'

'I have no intention of crying,' said Leonora stiffly, and burst into tears.

She hadn't wept like that for a long time, not since bouncer, the family cat, had died of old age, lying in the sun at the back of the house. She sobbed and sniffed, hardly aware that she was making a fine mess of the doctor's jacket, her head buried against his shoulder while she muttered and mumbled and wept.

Presently she lifted a sodden face. 'I'm so sorry; I really am. I never cry—well, almost never.'

'A mistake; there's nothing like it for relieving the feelings.'

His voice was kind and his arms comforting. 'Now mop up and sit down and tell me all about it.'

He offered a large white handkerchief and nodded to Cricket to put the coffee-tray down on a side table, then he went to the door and stood watching the two dogs, who were still cautiously getting to know each other, not looking at her, giving her time to wipe away her tears and tuck back her hair. She gave a final sniff. 'I'll let

you have your hanky back,' she told him. 'I'm quite all
right now.'

He poured their coffee and gave her a cup and offered
biscuits to the dogs.

'They seem to like each other,' said Leonora, anxious
to get the conversation onto an impersonal footing again.

'Naturally. They are intelligent animals.' He sat down
opposite her but not facing her directly. 'Begin at the
beginning, Leonora.'

'It's all so silly; I mean, I don't believe a word of it.
There must be some mistake.'

'If there is, we can, perhaps, discover it.' He was sitting back in his chair, quite at ease—a man, she reflected, who could solve the knottiest problem without
fuss.

'Well,' she began, and poured it all out in rather a
muddle, for, just for once, her common sense had for-
saken her. 'I simply can't understand why Tony has sent
these men. I'm quite sure he has said nothing to Father.
Besides, Father wouldn't even listen to a plan like
that—' she gulped '—to build houses on our land—and
where are we supposed to live? It doesn't make sense.'

It made sense to the doctor although he didn't say so.

'Would you like to go to London and talk to Tony?
Ask for an explanation? There may be a reason of which
you know nothing. Perhaps he intends to surprise you in
some way, but if you tell him that you are worried about
the rumours he will tell you what he has in mind. Since
he is to marry you, I imagine it is some scheme bene-
ficial to you and your parents.'

He didn't imagine anything of the kind—Tony
Beamish was capable of manipulating affairs to suit himself—but perhaps it wasn't as bad as Leonora thought it
was. After all, the man loved her, presumably; he

wouldn't want to hurt her in any way, even if it meant forgoing whatever ambitious plans he had.

Leonora said suddenly, 'I think you're right. I'll go up to town and see him. I'll not tell him I'm going. I've an aunt living in Chelsea—I can say I'm going to see her and go and see him after he gets back from work.'

'That sounds like a good idea. I have to go up to town myself tomorrow afternoon. I'll be there for a day or two. If you're ready to come back with me, well and good; otherwise you can get a train.'

'Thank you; I'd like that. I'll stay the night, perhaps two nights. I'm very grateful for your help.' She put down her coffee-cup. 'I'll go home...'

'I dare say you would like to wash your face first,' he observed in a matter-of-fact voice. 'Cricket will show you where to go.'

She was still pale when she rejoined him but quite composed. He doubted if her parents would notice anything amiss although Nanny probably would. She thanked Cricket for the coffee and waited while the doctor saw the dogs onto the back seat of the car.

As he drove the short distance to her home he told her, 'I'll be leaving around two o'clock—I'll call for you.'

At the house he got out to open her door and then allow a reluctant Wilkins to join her. 'You're quite sure that you want to go and see Beamish?'

She nodded. 'Oh, yes. Otherwise I'm going to fuss and fret, aren't I?'

He smiled down at her. 'You're a sensible woman, Leonora.'

After he had driven away she went slowly indoors, not sure that she liked being called 'a sensible woman' in that casual manner.

Her mother and father saw nothing unusual in her wish to visit Aunt Marion. 'A good idea, darling,' said her mother. 'It will make a nice change for you, and Aunt Marion loves company. Perhaps you'll see Tony. Don't stay too long, though; remember there's the village bazaar coming up and I've promised that we'll help—take a stall or something. Mrs Willoughby will tell you, I've no doubt. Lydia Dowling will be organising it so I expect you'll have to go to see her to talk about it.'

Nanny looked at Leonora sharply when she told her that she was going to visit her aunt for a day or two.

'A bit sudden, isn't it? Going to see that Mr Beamish, are you?'

'Well, yes, I expect so. Nanny, why don't you like him?'

Nanny bent over a saucepan, inspecting its contents. 'We all have our likes and dislikes,' she said reluctantly. 'I dare say I'll get around to liking him in a while.' She sniffed. 'Perhaps he'll improve with marriage.'

Leonora, packing an overnight bag later, hesitated as to what to take with her. She intended to see Tony on the following evening. There wouldn't be time to change when she reached her aunt's house but if she stayed for a second day she would need a dress, since Aunt Marion had old-fashioned notions about changing for dinner.

She crammed a stone-coloured jersey dress in with her night things and added a pair of high-heeled shoes. She would go in the tweed suit and easy shoes; both had seen better days but they had been good when new. Her handbag and gloves were beyond reproach. She had a very small income from a godmother's bequest—money she seldom touched, saving it for a rainy day. Well, that day had come; she would nip down to the village in the morning and get Mrs Pike to cash a cheque…

The doctor was punctual. He came into the house and spent five minutes talking to her mother and father before settling her in the car and getting in beside her. Beyond asking her if she was comfortable he had little to say as he drove along minor roads to reach the M4, and once on the motorway he shot smoothly ahead.

'Your aunt knows you are coming?'

'Yes, I phoned her last night. She's a very hospitable person and very sociable. She may not be there when I arrive but she has a marvellous housekeeper who's been with her for ages. I'm to stay for as long as I like.'

'Will you give me her phone number before I drop you off? I'll phone you when I'm ready to leave in case you would like a lift back.'

'That's very kind of you. I don't expect to be in London for more than a day or two. If Tony's free he might drive me home.' Before she could stop herself, she added, 'I'm sure it's a mistake—a misunderstanding. He'll explain…'

'There is always an explanation, Leonora, although sometimes we have to look for one. Will you see him this evening?'

'Yes, I'll go to his flat. I've never been there; it's in a street just off Curzon Street.'

The doctor raised his eyebrows. 'A very good address. He is a successful businessman, I should suppose.'

Somehow, talking about Tony made the whole puzzling business seem far-fetched. She said slowly, 'I wonder if I'm just being very silly…?'

'No. If the whole thing is, as you say, a misunderstanding, then the quicker it is put to rights the better.

Five minutes' talk together and probably you will both be laughing over the matter.'

'Yes, I'm sure you're right. Are you going to be busy while you're in London?'

'A seminar and a couple of lectures I want to attend, friends to look up. A theatre, perhaps.'

He would have friends, she reflected, and since he was single, handsome and an asset to any dinner table he would be much in demand. Besides, perhaps he would see this girl who had called his dog by such a silly name. She switched her thoughts away from that; it was none of her business what he did in his private life.

Her aunt lived in a narrow street of small but elegant houses; the doctor, following Leonora's directions calmly, drew up before its pristine door, flanked by two bay trees in tubs, and got out to open Leonora's door.

She got out, waited while he fetched her overnight bag from the boot and then held out a hand. 'Thank you very much,' she told him. 'I hope I haven't brought you too much out of your way.'

'No, no. I'll wait until you are indoors...'

Her aunt's housekeeper answered her knock and she turned to smile at him as she went inside.

Mrs Fletcher, the housekeeper, greeted her placidly. 'The mistress is out, miss; I'm to show you to your room and give you tea. Mrs Thurston will be back around six o'clock.'

So Leonora tidied herself in the charming room overlooking the tiny back garden and had her tea in the elegant sitting room.

Aunt Marion, a childless widow, had been left comfortably off by a doting husband, so that she lived pleasantly in her little gem of a house, surrounded by charming furniture and leading the kind of life she enjoyed—

shopping, bridge parties, theatres—at the same time retaining a warm heart and generous nature. Sir William was a good deal older than she and she saw very little of him, but years ago, when they were children, she had been his favourite sister, and still was.

She came home soon after Leonora had finished her tea, embraced her niece warmly and demanded to know why she had come on this unexpected visit.

'Not that I'm not delighted to have you, my dear— you know that—but it's not like you... Is there anything wrong at home?'

Leonora gave her reasons, carefully couched in neutral terms.

'Ah, yes, of course you must have a talk. The whole thing sounds preposterous to me, but I know what villages are—someone has got the wrong end of the stick.'

Leonora nodded, not at all certain about that; all the same, her aunt's bracing opinion put heart into her and when they had dined she declared her intention of going to Tony's flat.

'Now? Wouldn't you like to phone him first?'

'No, I don't think so. I mean, if I just walk in and ask him he'll tell me at once, if you see what I mean.'

Her aunt understood very well. She was another one who wasn't quite happy about Tony Beamish. Let the girl catch him on the hop, as it were!

'Take a taxi, dear,' she advised. 'Have you sufficient money?'

When the taxi stopped outside the block of flats where Tony lived, Leonora got out, paid the driver and stood a minute looking around her.

It was a dignified street, lined with large houses and sedate blocks of flats—the kind that had enormous porticos with a lot of glass and wrought iron and a uniformed man just inside the door. Tony had told her that he was on the first floor and she looked up as she reached the entrance, half expecting to see him at one of the windows.

The porter enquired whom she wished to visit and offered to phone Mr Beamish's flat and announce her.

She smiled at him. 'I'd rather you didn't; it's a surprise.' She declined the lift, walked up the wide stairs and knocked on the door bearing his name.

A sour-faced man opened it. She disliked him at once for no reason that she could think of and asked politely if she might see Mr Beamish.

'Tell him it is Miss Crosby,' she said, and went past him into a small hall, thickly carpeted, its walls hung with paintings and vases of flowers on the wall tables. A bit overdone, she thought, but probably Tony had a housekeeper as well as the sour-faced man. She sat down composedly on a small walnut hall chair and watched the door through which the man had gone.

Nothing happened for a few minutes, then the door was flung open and Tony came into the hall.

'What in heaven's name brings you here?' he demanded, and the happy excitement of seeing him again slowly shrivelled at the cold anger in his voice. He must have seen her face because he added quickly, 'Darling, what has happened? Is it your father—something dire?'

Leonora stayed on the chair. 'Hello, Tony. No, Father is very well. I want to talk to you.'

'My dear girl, why couldn't you have phoned?' He had controlled his annoyance now and bent to kiss her. 'I have guests—a dinner party. I simply can't leave them.' He glanced at the tweed suit and the sensible shoes. 'You aren't dressed...' he began.

Leonora got up. 'I'll come back tomorrow. Will you

be here in the evening? About six o'clock? I won't keep
you long and I shall be dining with Aunt Marion.'

'You do understand, Leonora? They're important people—colleagues in the business world.'

He kissed her again and she turned her cheek away
and walked to the door. 'I'll see you tomorrow,' she told
him in a rather small, polite voice, and went past the
sour-faced man, who had appeared to open the door, and
down the stairs.

At the entrance she asked the porter to get her a taxi,
stood quietly until it arrived, then tipped the man and
got in, outwardly serene while her thoughts were in
chaos. Tony hadn't been pleased to see her; surely if he
loved her he would have been only too glad to see her?
She thought he had looked furiously angry; he had been,
for a moment, a man she didn't know.

Her aunt was out when she got back, which meant
that she could go to bed early, pleading tiredness after
her journey—something which the housekeeper found
understandable. Not that Leonora slept, not until the
small hours. She pondered her few minutes with Tony,
and because she loved him—well, she was going to
marry him, wasn't she? So she must love him—she sup-
pressed the doubt at once and convinced herself that he
had been tired after his day's work. It had been her fault;
she should have warned him of her coming. She must
learn to accommodate her actions to suit his... She slept
at last on this high-minded resolve.

In the morning, yesterday evening's meeting faded
into something which had been regrettable and entirely
her fault, and hard on this thought there followed the
one that Tony would certainly have an explanation for
the goings-on in the village.

She spent the morning at Harrods with her aunt, pretending that she had all the clothes she wanted while her aunt tried on hats, and in the afternoon she made a fourth at bridge, a game at which she was only tolerably good. However, since her aunt had been so kind as to have her for a guest, she could do no other than express pleasure at the prospect of several hours of anxious concentration.

They played for money too but, as Aunt Marion explained laughingly, the stakes would be very low, otherwise it wouldn't be fair to rob her niece.

Kindly fate allowed Leonora and her partner, a formidable dowager in a towering hat, to win as often as they lost, so that she was a little better off by the time they stopped for tea.

Then it was time for her to go and see Tony once more.

# CHAPTER FIVE

THE sour-faced man admitted Leonora when she reached Tony's flat. This time he led her through the hall and into a large room overlooking the street. It was splendidly furnished and its tall windows were elaborately curtained but she hardly noticed this. Tony was coming towards her, his arms outstretched.

'Darling, how lovely to see you. I am so sorry about yesterday evening. Sometimes the only chance I have to discuss things with colleagues is over a meal. Come and sit down and tell me why you wanted to see me so urgently!'

He went to a small table against one wall. 'What would you like to drink?' He glanced over his shoulder. 'I have to go out shortly—you said you were dining with your aunt so I saw no reason to cancel it.'

'No, of course not.' All the same she felt chilled by his remark. It was as if he was fitting her in between more important engagements. She refused a drink and told herself not to be petty.

He came and sat down opposite her. 'This is delightful,' he told her, smiling. 'I have so often sat here and wished that you were here with me.' He sat back, at his ease. 'Now, what's all this about?'

She went straight to the point, already feeling confident that the whole business was a storm in a teacup.

'There are two men staying at the Blue Man; they have been asking questions—searching questions—about the house and our park. Two days ago I was told that they were there on behalf of someone who intends to buy the house and the land and build houses on it, as well as restoring the house. I was told that the someone was you, Tony.'

He was no longer smiling. His face was coldly angry and he didn't look at her.

'It's true,' said Leonora in a quiet voice. 'Why, Tony? Tell me why and perhaps I'll understand.'

He was smiling again, even laughing a little. 'Listen, darling. Your father's house needs to be restored; it's already half a ruin—no paintwork, faulty plumbing, doors broken, windows warped, floors uneven, brick-work crumbling. I intend to restore it and modernise it at the same time—new bathrooms, carpets, curtains, wallpapers, the lot.

'We will live on the top floor—a flat with its own entrance, of course—the rest will be used as a business centre. You have no idea of the number of clients I have who come here from Japan, the Middle East, the Continent. It's an ideal spot for them to come for conferences, make decisions, arrange mergers. It'll be run at a profit—I'll see to that.

'And yes, the park is useless as it is; the land will bring in a splendid amount of money and the village will benefit from an influx of new inhabitants. They will be decent-sized places and the people who buy them will bring money with them—the village will love that. Of course I'll see that your father and mother have a suitable house—something that gorgon of a nanny can run single-handed—and of course I'll see that your father is financially comfortable.'

Leonora, listening to this rigmarole, couldn't believe her ears. Rage had kept her silent—a rage strong enough to make her forget that her world was tumbling round her. Now she asked quietly, 'Is this why you wanted to marry me? So that you could do all this?'

She showed no sign of her strong feelings. so Tony said lightly, 'Well, I must admit that that was one of the reasons…'

'There must be any number of girls like me,' said Leonora, 'with elderly parents living in dilapidated old houses; you shouldn't have much difficulty in finding one.'

She stood up, took the ring off her finger and laid it gently on the table by her chair. 'I'm not going to marry you, Tony. I never want to see you again, and if you don't recall those men and drop the whole idea I shall get our solicitor to take the matter up.' She walked to the door. 'You're ruthless and wicked and greedy; I'msurprised that I didn't see that. Luckily I do now.'

He crossed the room and caught her arm. 'Leonora, darling, you can't go like this; I've taken you by surprise. Go away and think about it. 'It's a splendid scheme and you'll benefit from it—everything you could ever want.'

She turned to look at him. 'All I ever want is to live at Pont Magna amongst friends and people I've known all my life.'

'But you love me—'

'I thought I did, but there's a difference.'

She gave him a little nod and went into the hall and through the door, which the sour-faced man had opened. She walked down the stairs, bade the porter a polite goodnight, asked him to get her a taxi and when it came got in.

When she got out at her aunt's house she was so white that the driver asked her if she felt ill and only drove away when she assured him that there was nothing wrong. She said the same to Mrs Fletcher and followed her obediently into the drawing room, feeling peculiar. I mustn't faint or cry, she thought.

Her aunt was there, sitting by the small, bright fire, and standing at the window was Dr Galbraith. They turned to look at her as she went in and she stood just inside the door, knowing that if she said anything she would burst into tears. But they had seen her face and understood.

'Come and sit down, Leonora,' said her aunt. 'Mrs Fletcher's bringing coffee. I'm sure you can do with a cup.'

So she sat down, still without speaking, until she asked in a tight voice, 'Why are you here, Doctor?'

He came and sat down, half turned away from her. 'I phoned to see if you wanted a lift home and Mrs Thurston suggested that I might come and wait for you here.'

'Oh—oh, I see. That's very kind of you...'

'Would you like to go home?' The casual friendliness of his voice was comforting.

She looked at her aunt.

'You would like it, wouldn't you, Leonora? Why not? You may be sure that I understand, my dear; you don't have to tell me anything.'

'Thank you, Aunt Marion. I'd like to go home very much if you don't mind. I—that is, Tony and I aren't getting married so I don't need to stay. It was very kind of you to have me... You don't think I'm rude? I don't mean to be!'

'Bless you, girl, of course I don't. I'd do the same in your shoes. Here's the coffee; drink it while it's hot, while Mrs Fletcher packs your bag for you. You'll be home by bedtime. So convenient that Dr Galbraith should be going back this evening.'

'Two days here is enough for me,' observed the doctor, which led to an exchange of views about London versus the country while Leonora drank her coffee, swallowing with it the tears she longed to shed.

Ten minutes later she wished her aunt goodbye and got into the car, her pretty face set in a rigid smile while she uttered her thanks once more.

'In a day or so, when you've had a good cry and found that life's worth living after all, you shall tell me all about it,' said Aunt Marion.

As he drove away the doctor observed casually, 'What a very sensible and delightful woman your aunt is. Do you want to phone your mother?'

'No, I don't think so; she might worry and wonder why I'm coming back...'

'We should be home well before bedtime. We'll stop on the way and have a meal.'

'I'm not hungry.'

He ignored that. 'There's rather a nice pub in a village just off the motorway once we've passed Reading. That should suit us nicely. There's plenty of time for you to have a good cry before we get there, and if I remember rightly the lighting is very dim there.'

She didn't know whether to laugh or cry. 'You think of everything,' she told him. 'I'd much rather go straight home.'

'Of course you would, but consider, Leonora. The moment you entered the door you would burst into tears, upset the household and make a complete muddle of explaining.'

She took an indignant breath. 'What a horrid thing to

say. You seem to forget that I'm a grown woman and perfectly able to control myself.'

He said placidly, 'Well, it will take a little while to get to this pub; you can think about it and tell me what you want to do when we reach the turn-off.'

He had no more to say then, which meant that she had no way of ignoring her thoughts, so that presently her much vaunted self-control collapsed and she sat rigid while the tears rolled down her cheeks. It seemed that nothing would stop them; she looked sideways out of the window although it was already getting dark and there was nothing to see, swallowing the sobs.

They were bypassing Reading when the doctor handed her his handkerchief.

'Shall we go to the pub?' he asked with brisk friend-liness.

She mopped her face, blew her pretty nose and said, 'Yes, please, only I must look a fright...'

'Does that matter? No one will know you there and they will be locals chatting over their pints—and I don't mind what you look like.'

Despite her misery, Leonora took exception to that remark.

The village was four or five miles off the motorway, a handful of cottages, one or two handsome houses and the church, and opposite it the pub—a quite small place with a solid door and small windows.

The doctor had been quite right—it was indeed dimly lit and, although the bar was almost full, beyond a quick glance no one bothered to really look at them. Moreover, at one end of the bar there were tables, none of them occupied. He led her to a small table under the window.

'I'll fetch our drinks and see what we can have to eat. If you want the Ladies it is in that far corner.'

He sounded exactly as she imagined a brother would sound—unfussed and casual. She nodded and took herself off and found the light in the cloakroom, unlike the one in the bar, was so powerful that it could show every wrinkle. No wrinkles in her case but certainly a rather tear-stained face, fortunately not beyond repair. She emerged presently, feeling a good deal better, and found the doctor sitting at the table reading the menu.

He got up as she reached him. 'I'd like you to drink what's in that glass,' he told her, 'and no arguing.'

'What is it?'

She took a sip since he didn't answer and said, 'Oh. Brandy, isn't it?'

He nodded. 'I am sure you would have liked a pot of tea—we'll have that later.'

She eyed his own glass. 'That looks like water...'

'Bottled water. I'm driving. Now, we have quite a choice.' He handed her the menu. 'Last time I was here I had a jacket potato piled high with baked beans—it was delicious. Soup first? No? Then I'll order.'

He wandered over to the bar, gave his order, stopped to exchange a few cheerful comments with the men there and then wandered back again.

'Drink your brandy and then start at the beginning. Never mind if it's all a bit muddled; the thing is to get it off your chest so that you can think clearly about what you want to do next.'

She said tartly, 'You sound like an agony aunt in a women's magazine...'

'God forbid, but I do have five sisters. I grew up steeped, as it were, in the female sex. In a position to offer humble advice if asked for it.'

She said quickly, 'That was a horrid thing I said about

being an agony aunt. I'm sorry. I'm sure you must be a very nice brother.'

'Thank you. And now, having established my suitability as confidant, tell me what has happened to bring about this unfortunate situation.'

The brandy had been a great help. She related the whole sorry business in a voice which only wobbled occasionally and while she talked she ate the potato and beans with an appetite she hadn't realised she had.

The doctor said nothing at all, not even when she stopped to subdue a particularly persistent wobble. It wasn't until they had finished and a pot of tea and cups and saucers had been set before them that he observed, 'There is a possibility that Beamish will come hotfoot after you, beg your forgiveness and scrap his plans. Have you considered that he might have had the best intentions?'

Leonora gave him a cold look. 'He said one of the reasons for marrying me was so that he could get his hands on the house and land.' She drew a furious breath, looking quite beautiful despite the slightly reddened nose.

'I'm not sure any more if he ever loved me. How can I be?'

The doctor sighed gently. It would be tragic if young Beamish could persuade her into thinking that the whole thing had been nothing but a misunderstanding—something he would be quite capable of doing—and it would be easy if he himself dropped sufficient hints as to the man's character to put her on her guard, but he had no right to interfere. In any case, he reminded himself, Leonora was no shy young girl; she must decide for herself what she wanted from life.

'I think that perhaps you will know that when you see

him again.' At her look of doubt he added, 'Oh, you will, you know. You must follow your heart, Leonora.'

Back in the car, speeding along the motorway once more, sitting in a friendly silence, Leonora thought about the doctor's advice. It had been sound, unbiased and quite impersonal. She would take it, only she wished that he had been a little more sympathetic. There was no reason why he should be, she reminded herself; he had given her advice just as, doubtless, he gave advice to such of his patients who asked for it.

The lights were still on at the house when he drew up before it. He got out to open her door and said, 'I'll come in with you,' and she gave him a grateful look.

'I've my key,' she told him, and they went in together just as Nanny came into the hall from the kitchen end.

'Well, I must say that seeing you so sudden is a bit of a shock. You didn't phone.' She looked at the doctor as she spoke.

'Hello, Nanny,' said Leonora. 'I'm sorry if we made you jump. Dr Galbraith gave me a lift home. Are Mother and Father in the drawing room?'

Nanny nodded. 'You could do with a cup of coffee, the pair of you. I'll bring it presently.'

Lady Crosby was doing a jigsaw puzzle and Sir William was reading. It was Wilkins who came to meet them as they went in, delighted to see them.

'Leonora—we didn't expect you—you haven't phoned.' Her mother looked surprised. 'And Dr Galbraith.' She frowned. 'Tony isn't with you?' She glanced at her husband. 'Your father and I thought he might come back with you—you must have seen him.'

Her father had put down his book. 'Something's wrong?' he asked.

'I went to London to see Tony about something—

something I had been told about him. We—that is, I decided that I don't want to marry him so we're not engaged any more.'

'There's more to it than that,' Sir William said sharply.

'Yes, but it can wait until tomorrow morning, Father. I had the chance to come back with Dr Galbraith. He most kindly gave me a lift.'

'Much obliged to you,' said her father. 'Come and sit down; I'm sure Nanny will have made us coffee.' He turned his head. 'Leonora, run and tell Nanny to bring it as soon as it's ready.'

When she had gone, relieved to be away from her mother's faint air of disapproval, he asked, 'All right, is she? More to it than she has said—'

'Yes, a good deal more, Sir William, but I am sure that Leonora will explain everything later. She has had a very trying time and she is tired.'

Sir William nodded. 'Then we won't pester her this evening. Good of you to bring her back. You know what happened, of course?'

The doctor looked grim. 'Yes, indeed I do.'

Leonora came in with the coffee-tray then, and after ten minutes or so of desultory talk the doctor got up to go.

Leonora went with him to the door. 'Thank you again,' she said, and offered a hand. 'And thank you for listening. You were quite right—it's much easier to think sensibly now I've talked about it. You didn't mind?'

He was still holding her hand. 'No, Leonora, I didn't mind. I hope that if you should need a shoulder to cry on at any time you'll use mine.'

He gave her a brotherly thump on the shoulder and went out to his car and drove away.

Once she was back in the drawing room her mother said with a little *moue* of discontent, 'Your father says we are to wait until tomorrow before you tell us exactly what has happened to bring you rushing back like this. You say you are no longer engaged to Tony… You must have a very good reason—'

Sir William said sharply, 'That is enough, my dear; Leonora is tired; no doubt she has had a long day with things to worry her. She should go to bed and in the morning, if she wishes, she will tell us what happened.'

So Leonora went thankfully to bed and rather to her surprise went to sleep at once, to wake the next morning feeling that she was able to cope with the situation and determined that if Tony should want to see her she would refuse.

That would be the only way, she reflected as she dressed and went downstairs to the kitchen, for if they were to meet again she wasn't sure if she could withstand his charm, despite knowing now that he had never really loved her—not with the kind of love she wanted. He had thought of her as someone who went with the house and the land, someone he would possibly treat with casual affection, load with jewellery and dress in lovely clothes and who would be expected to agree to all his plans.

'Well, I won't,' said Leonora, putting on the kettle, and she wished Nanny a good morning. She opened the door for Wilkins and stood taking great breaths of the early-morning air.

'And what's all this I hear from your ma?' asked Nanny.

Leonora fetched a teapot and spooned in the tea. 'I haven't explained yet,' she said, 'and I'll tell you all about it, Nanny, but first I have to tell Father and Mother.'

Which, over the breakfast table, proved a difficult task. Her father stared with disbelief.

'This house? My land? The park? I cannot believe it, Leonora…'

'No, I know it's difficult, Father, but it's true. Tony had it all planned—you and Mother were to be moved to a smaller house—'

'I could not possibly live in a small house,' observed her mother, 'and what about the Sheraton chairs and the William and Mary display cabinet? And the other furniture—it would never fit into a small house. I think it was most inconsiderate of him to even suggest such a thing. Why were we not told?'

Sir William asked, 'These men staying in the village—you say that Tony sent them? Leonora, I find this very difficult to believe.'

'So did I, Father, but it's true. I told Tony that he was to recall the men and that there was no question of you selling the house and the land.'

'Quite right too, my dear.' Sir William, not the most sensitive of men, all the same added, 'I hope this hasn't upset you too much, Leonora.'

'I expect I'm as upset as any woman who expects to get married and then finds that she won't after all,' said Leonora.

Lady Crosby wiped away a tear. 'And I was planning the wedding. What will everyone think…?'

'I don't care what they think,' said Leonora with a snap, and took herself off to the kitchen before she lost her cool and burst into tears.

It was all right to cry against Nanny's elderly shoulder, pouring out her rage and disappointment and un-

happiness in a jumble of words. She felt better then and
sat down at the table with Wilkins pressed against her
and drank the tea Nanny had made.

'He'll come after you,' said Nanny. 'If he wants the
house and the land he'll not give them up without another try. And if you truly love him, dearie, it won't
matter what he's done; you'll forgive him and he'll get
his way. Even Sir William would give in eventually once
you were wed and Tony could show him a good reason
for parting with the house and giving it to you—and to
him, of course.'

'I won't listen to him; I never want to see him
again...'

'I dare say you'll have to, Miss Leonora; you can't
run away if he comes here. Besides, you may have got
over your rage by then and discovered that you love him
enough to want to have him back.'

Leonora drank her tea. 'Nanny, have you ever been
in love?'

'Bless the girl, of course I have. He was a deep-sea
fisherman—drowned, he was, years ago now. But we
were in love and we loved each other. Being in love is
one thing—it doesn't always last, but loving does.'

'Nanny, I didn't know. I'm so sorry. You never
wanted to marry after that?'

'What for? I never met a man to touch my Ned.'

Nanny got to her feet. 'I'm going up to make the beds,
if you'll tidy the drawing room. You'll be going to the
village presently?'

'Yes, we want one or two things, don't we? I'm not
sure what happens next.'

'Sir William will know what to do.'

Leonora hoovered and dusted and listened to her
mother's gentle complaining. 'Of course,' she said,

'Tony is sure to come here and want to see you and no doubt explain everything.' Lady Crosby blew her nose daintily and glanced at Leonora. 'After all, he does love you.' She frowned at Leonora's wooden expression. 'Well, he does, doesn't he?'

'I think,' said Leonora carefully, 'that he loves this house and the land, and because he can only get them if I make up the package, as it were, he may be a little in love with me.'

'But you love him, darling?'

Leonora dusted a fragile porcelain figurine with great care. 'I'm not sure, Mother.'

Mrs Pike's shop was empty when Leonora went in, the faithful Wilkins at her heels. She gave her order and nibbled at the biscuit she was offered—a new line in slimming rusks—while Mrs Pike collected tea, sugar, rice and corned beef.

'They've gone,' she said, leaning over the counter and speaking in a loud whisper just as though they were surrounded by eavesdroppers. 'Them men at the Blue Man. Went first thing this morning. Had a phone call from London last night. Pike happened to be in the bar and couldn't help but hear. Very surprised they were too.'

Leonora finished the rusk. 'I'm not surprised; I saw Mr Beamish yesterday and—the matter has been settled.'

She took off a glove to tuck her hair back and Mrs Pike said sharply, 'Your ring, Miss Crosby—lost it, have you?'

Leonora went pink. 'No—no, Mr Beamish and I are not to be married after all.'

Mrs Pike wordlessly handed her another biscuit. 'Well, I never...and it were a whopping great diamond.'

'Yes, it was, wasn't it?' Leonora found to her surprise

that she didn't mind not having it. On second thoughts she wasn't even sure that she liked diamonds.

She went back home presently and found her father in his study.

'They've gone, the two men.' She told him what Mrs Pike had said and then said, 'Father, do you suppose that Tony will want to see me or you and explain?'

'Yes, I do, my dear. You do not need to see him on your own unless you want to. I shall certainly want an explanation and an apology.'

There was no sign of Tony, however. No letter, no telephone call. After several days, Leonora stopped listening for the phone and looking through the post each morning, nor did she catch her breath each time a car went past the gates. She had phoned Aunt Marion to thank her for her visit and that lady had informed her that Tony had made no attempt to get in touch with her. 'Although why he should wish to do so I'm sure I don't know.'

The doctor, kept up to date with village gossip by Cricket, whose benevolent and discreet manner had quite won over the hearts and the confidences of the village ladies, knew better. Tony Beamish was no fool; he would bide his time, wait until Leonora had had the time to realise that her future was no longer the one she had been looking forward to. He was a conceited man and very sure of himself; he would bank on Leonora missing him and everything he stood for and at the right moment he would turn up to beg forgiveness and convince her that everything would be changed. If she loved him he would eventually get what he wanted.

He could do nothing about it, of course. Leonora wasn't some young, empty-headed girl; she could think for herself. All he could do was listen if she needed to talk.

It was a pity that he saw no sign of her for several days. He had a number of patients living on outlying farms and the surgery at that time of year was full with nasty chests, flu and a mild outbreak of chickenpox amongst the small fry. He drove to Bath to see Ben but, passing the gates to her home, he could see no sign of anyone.

Which was a shame, for Leonora needed to talk to someone. Her parents, outraged at Tony's behaviour, didn't wish to discuss the matter, and Nanny, friend and confidante though she was, had declared that she was in no position to give advice.

Tony arrived on Monday, ten days after Leonora had seen him in London. He drove up to the house, got out and looked it over before ringing the bell. Despite its shabby appearance, it was a lovely old place and he had no intention of giving it up lightly.

When Leonora opened the door he said eagerly, 'Hello, darling. Have you calmed down enough for us to have a talk? You didn't mean it, you know.' He smiled with charm. 'I've brought the ring with me...'

Leonora stood in the doorway, blocking his path.

'I've calmed down and I meant it,' she said, 'so you can go away again.'

He put a hand on her arm. 'You don't mean that, Leonora. Think of all the marvellous things you will miss—I'll be good to you—'

'No, you won't,' said Leonora. 'I don't want anything more to do with you, and if Father hears any more about your plans he intends to get our solicitor to deal with it.'

Tony laughed. 'I say—look here, old girl, you don't

mean that. You can't have thought about it—the advantages…'

'To you, yes. Have you come to see Father?'

'No, no. At least, I thought if I saw you first then we might see him together and explain.'

'Explain what? That you deceived him as well as me? Go away, Tony.'

'I'm not going until we've had a talk, until I've been given the chance to explain.'

Leonora, not the nervous type, nevertheless didn't like the look on his face, and he had put his foot in the door so that shutting it in his face was no longer possible. I need help, she thought.

She got it. Dr Galbraith, on his way back from Bath, glanced as he always did at the house as he passed. He slowed, reversed and slid silently up the drive to the door. His good morning was uttered in a genial voice. 'As I was passing I thought I might just take a look at your father.'

He had, without apparent effort, got between Leonora and Tony and turned to smile at him now. 'Rather unexpected, isn't it?' he wanted to know cheerfully. 'You're not very popular around here, you know.' He shook his head in a disapproving fashion. 'You have got yourself a very bad name in the village.' He looked at Leonora. 'Is he bothering you, Leonora?'

At her eloquent look he added, 'If you've come to make your peace with Sir William I strongly advise against it. The best thing you can do, my dear chap, is to go back to wherever you came from and stay there!'

Tony found his voice. 'What business is it of yours? This is a private matter between Leonora and myself.'

The doctor shook his head. 'You're mistaken, Beamish; there's nothing private about it. The Crosbys have been here for a couple of hundred years, they're part of the village life, and, believe me, you haven't a single friend in Pont Magna.'

He smiled pleasantly but his eyes were blue ice and Tony was the first to look away. 'Don't think I am going to be intimidated by threats—' he began.

'Threats? No one is threatening you, Beamish—a friendly warning, perhaps.'

'There is no point in staying here,' said Tony. 'I shall come back when there is a chance to talk to you privately, darling.'

'Don't you "darling" me,' said Leonora frostily. 'I don't want to see you again and that is the last time I'll say it.'

'But you love me...' Tony infused a cajoling note into his voice.

'No, I don't. I thought I did, but I don't.'

A remark which the doctor found most satisfactory. Leonora was too good for that fellow, he reflected; some decent chap would come along and marry her sooner or later.

He watched Beamish go to his car and get in and drive away and then said briskly, 'Well, now that that's sorted out, shall I see your father?'

She had expected him to say something soothing, express satisfaction at the way she had dealt with Tony. She turned on her heel and led the way indoors, feeling hurt.

'I'm sure he'll be pleased to see you, Doctor,' she observed in a cool voice. 'I'll bring coffee; Father usually has a cup about now.'

She put her head round the study door. 'Father, here's Dr Galbraith to see you.'

Her father lowered *The Times*. 'Ask him to come in. I heard someone—I was wondering who it was.'

She stood aside to let the doctor pass then went into the kitchen and thumped cups and saucers down on a tray, knocked over the sugar bowl and used what Nanny called 'unsuitable language'.

'What's upset you, Miss Leonora?' asked her old friend. 'Who was that at the door? Leaving someone at the door is bad manners.'

'It was Tony Beamish and he did upset me and I had no intention of letting him come into the house,' said Leonora pettishly. 'Dr Galbraith's here; I'm taking coffee to the study. Where's Mother?'

'Up in her room, going through her wardrobe. A good thing too.'

Leonora found biscuits and put them on a plate and Nanny asked, 'That Tony of yours...?'

'He's not mine.'

'Good thing too. Making trouble, is he?'

'No—well, he wanted me to be engaged again.' She poured the coffee. 'Actually, he got a bit—well, awkward, but Dr Galbraith was passing and stopped.'

Nanny nodded in a satisfied way. 'And sent him right about.'

'Well, yes, but quite nicely, if you see what I mean.'

'Yes, I see,' said Nanny. 'Will you take a cup of coffee up to your mother when you come back?'

The two men were sitting chatting comfortably. The doctor got up and took the tray from Leonora as she went in but she didn't look at him as she went away again.

Her mother, occupied with her clothes, greeted her absent-mindedly.

'I do need new clothes,' she said plaintively. 'Did I hear someone talking in the hall?'

'Dr Galbraith is with Father. He called in as he was passing.'

'I'll come down and see him—perhaps he can give me something; I feel I need a change—a little holiday, perhaps, a few days in town with your aunt Marion. Breaking off your engagement to Tony has been a great disappointment to me, Leonora.'

'It was rather a disappointment to me, Mother.'

'Yes, dear, of course, and I suppose he has behaved very badly. Never mind, there are plenty more fish in the sea.'

'Perhaps I'm not a very good angler,' said Leonora, and went back to the kitchen.

She was still there, peeling potatoes with unnecessary ferocity, when the doctor came in.

'There you are. I've been talking to your mother; she feels rather under the weather, she tells me. I've written a prescription for her; may I leave it with you, Leonora?' He watched her face. 'Your father is very well. How about you?'

'I never need the doctor,' said Leonora, and began on another potato.

He smiled. 'Don't tempt fate,' he said, and went away as quietly as he had come.

# CHAPTER SIX

AT LUNCH Lady Crosby said happily, 'Dr Galbraith has invited us to dine—rather short notice but he has friends coming down from London and he thought we might like to meet them. Next Saturday.'

Leonora remembered how she had sniffed and sobbed and made a fool of herself with the doctor. She said now, 'I'll have to refuse, Mother. I promised weeks ago that I'd babysit for Maggie—she and Gordon are going up to town to celebrate their anniversary. I said I'd spend the night.'

'For heaven's sake!' Her mother sounded impatient. 'They have a nursemaid, haven't they?'

'Yes, but she is very young and quite untrained. Did you accept for me as well as you and Father?'

'Yes, of course I did. Such a nice man, well connected too, and wealthy, I hear.'

'I'll write him a note,' said Leonora.

Which she did—a formal message of regret, couched in polite terms, which he read with some amusement and interest over his breakfast.

'Now why has she done that?' he enquired of the faithful Tod. 'Even if she had to refuse she could have phoned me or even called in at the surgery. We are, I suspect, to be Dr Galbraith and Miss Leonora Crosby again. A strange girl!'

He forgot about her then.

However, Leonora, who should by rights have been eating her heart out for the treacherous Tony, found herself thinking about the doctor. She liked him; he would be a splendid friend and she enjoyed his company and his matter-of-fact way of accepting events without fuss. But there was this vexed question of this young lady for whom he had a strong affection and, worse than that, her mother was making no secret of the fact that she would like it if Leonora and Dr Galbraith were to see more of each other. She would have to avoid him.

Luckily there would be a lot to do organising the fête, traditionally held in the park every year. Everyone had a hand in it, the practical making marmalade, cakes and sweets, embroidering small useless cushions and night-dress cases, knitting baby jackets, and the artistic painting local scenes.

Leonora, who drew and painted rather nicely, decided to shut herself in one of the attics and set to work. When she wasn't doing that she could go along to the Dowlings' and help with the writing of price tickets.

She took herself off to Maggie and Gordon's little house at the end of the village on Saturday afternoon and presently waved them goodbye as they drove off.

The house was charming, comfortably furnished and untidy. Leonora took her overnight bag up to the little guest room, had a chat with Sadie, the little nursery maid, and went about the business of making up feeds for three-month-old Tom. He was a placid baby, sleeping and feeding in a manner which would have delighted any writer of a childcare textbook.

The afternoon went by quickly, with a brisk walk in his pram, and feeding and bathing while Sadie got their tea and supper. And since Tom took his feed like a lamb at ten o'clock Leonora and Sadie went to bed and slept peacefully until the early morning.

It was a bright, chilly morning, and Leonora, sitting

by the window in the little nursery, giving Tom his bottle, was content. It would be delightful to have a baby of her own, she reflected, small and cuddly like Tom— several babies in fact. If she had married Tony... She wondered then if he would have liked children. Certainly he wouldn't have had much time for them.

'I should like a husband,' she told Tom, 'who would get up in the night if the baby cried and who'd bring me a cup of tea without being asked and wouldn't mind babies dribbling onto his shoulder. He'd play cricket with the little boys and comfort the little girls when they cried...'

She tickled Tom under his chin to encourage him to finish his bottle. 'You don't have to listen to my nonsense,' she assured him. 'We'll go for a walk and blow away the cobwebs.'

She had enjoyed her day, she reflected as she walked home after Maggie and Gordon had returned. Sadie had had tea ready for them and she had sat listening to their account of their day, before bidding Tom a reluctant goodbye.

'He was so good,' she assured her friend. 'I'll babysit any time that you want me to.'

Her mother and father were in the drawing room, he behind the Sunday papers and her mother sitting at a small table with a half-finished jigsaw puzzle.

'Enjoyed yourself?' asked her father, glancing up.

She bent to kiss his cheek. 'Yes, thank you, Father. Little Tom is a darling baby and so good.'

Her mother turned away impatiently from the puzzle. 'Darling, such a pity you couldn't come with us yesterday. I must say Dr Galbraith has a lovely house; I quite envy him some of his furniture—handed down in the family, I should think. There is a bow-fronted cabinet in the drawing room... And that man of his—Cricket—the kind of servant one dreams of and never finds! Dinner was excellent and these friends of his very pleasant. Ackroyd is the name—and funnily enough Mr Ackroyd knew your father's brother-in-law, Aunt Marion's husband, you know—when he was alive. She was quite nice too—rather quiet, but friendly enough. A good deal older than Dr Galbraith but I believe their daughter and he are on good terms. He should marry, of course.'

'I dare say he will, when he wants to,' said Leonora. 'I'm glad you enjoyed the evening.'

She wandered off to the kitchen and found Nanny cutting up vegetables for soup. Into her willing ears Leonora poured every small detail of little Tom's day. 'He's such a darling baby, Nanny, and so good.'

She ate a carrot and went out into the garden, having called Wilkins, and then beyond into the park, feeling restless. She had, she supposed, got used to the idea of marrying Tony in the not too distant future—a future she had taken for granted. Now the future stretched ahead of her empty, and just for the moment there seemed little purpose in it. She had been happily filling in time, helping to organise various village functions, accompanying her parents to friends' houses for dinner, summer picnics and winter bridge afternoons, but now these seemed a waste of time.

What else could she do? For a few years after she had left school she had travelled a little, visited friends, spent a week or two with Aunt Marion going to theatres, dancing, shopping. Since her father had lost his money, though, none of these things had been possible and she'd found herself more and more involved in coping with the running of the house since Nanny was the only other person to do that.

She couldn't blame her mother, who had never done the household chores and had very little idea of what they involved anyway. It looked as though she was destined to stay at home, getting longer and longer in the tooth, making do with too little money, doing the odd repairs, and painting in an amateurish way.

She jumped across the little stream which ran along the boundary of the park and wandered into the woods beyond while Wilkins padded to and fro. When he stood still and began to bark she paused too.

'What's up, Wilkins? Rabbits?'

It was very quiet under the trees but presently she heard footsteps—unhurried and deliberate—and Wilkins raced back the way they had come to meet them. Leonora stayed where she was; it was someone the dog knew and liked and for a moment she wondered if it was Tony but then dismissed the thought; Wilkins and Tony had never been more than guarded in their approach to each other.

Perhaps it was Dr Galbraith…

It was. He came towards her, still unhurried, Wilkins jumping up on his elderly legs and running in circles around him. His, 'Hello, Leonora,' was casual and friendly. 'I should have brought Tod with me…

'Nanny told me that you might be here.' He had reached her by now and strolled along beside her. 'There is something about which I wish to talk.'

'What?' asked Leonora baldly.

'Mrs Crisp has broken her arm. Would you consider taking over from her from the time being, a few weeks? Morning surgery is half past eight until eleven o'clock or thereabouts. Evening surgery five o'clock until seven—sometimes later. No surgery on Saturday evenings or Sunday.'

Leonora had listened with her mouth open. 'I can't type,' she managed. 'I don't know anything…'

'You know everyone in the village and for miles around. You know where people live, the jobs they have. You can answer the phone intelligently and not fly into hysterics if something crops up. It's an easy job for you. If I have to get someone from an agency they won't know their way around or where the patients live.'

Leonora closed her mouth at last. 'But I can't. I mean, I do most of the housekeeping at home and the shopping—and odd jobs around the place.'

'You would be paid like anyone else who works for a living. Surely there is someone in the village who could go to the house each day and give Nanny a hand?'

When she hesitated he added, 'You would be working—let me see—between twenty and thirty hours a week. There's a standard rate of pay.' He mentioned a sum which caused her mouth to drop open again.

'All that?' asked Leonora. She paused just long enough to do some most satisfying mental arithmetic. 'If you think I'll do I'll come and work for you.'

'Good. Now that's settled, how about coming back with me and I'll explain just what you have to do?'

'Well, yes, all right. I'd better take Wilkins back home first and tell Mother.'

He walked back with her, saying little, not mentioning the job again until they were in the house once more. As they went in through the garden door he asked, 'Do you want me to come with you?'

She considered this. 'Well, it might be a good idea.' She glanced at him. 'If you see what I mean?'

He nodded gravely. That the daughter of the house should have a job was something Lady Crosby wouldn't allow, but as a favour to the local doctor, an emergency, as it were—that would be a different matter.'

So it proved to be. Leonora could not help but admire the way in which the doctor convinced her mother that working for him at the surgery wasn't so much a job as a vital service to the community and that Leonora, being known in the village, was exactly the right person to undertake it.

'Well, I do see that as a member of the family Leonora has a certain duty. I mean, we have lived here for very many years, as you must know. I am sure it is a worthwhile undertaking since Mrs Crisp is unable to work for you.'

Lady Crosby frowned suddenly. 'There is one drawback—Leonora has undertaken the running of this house. I am rather delicate myself, Dr Galbraith; my poor health does not allow me to exert myself.'

She sighed. 'Such a pity, but I do not see how we are to manage if Leonora is away for most of the day.'

'Perhaps that is a problem which can be solved. Leonora will, of course, receive a salary. There must be someone in the village who would come here and work with Nanny while Leonora is away.'

Lady Crosby brightened. 'Well, yes. You say she will receive a salary?' She turned to look at the silent Leonora. 'That will be nice, my dear. I'm sure if you can find someone suitable to replace you for the time being neither your father nor I will have any objection to you helping the doctor.'

She smiled at him. 'You will stay to dinner? We dine late on Sundays.'

He refused with easy good manners and added, 'Perhaps I might take Leonora with me for an hour or so? I can give her some idea of her duties and we might share supper at the same time. The sooner she is able to start work, the better for me and my patients.'

'Yes, yes, of course. I can quite see that the matter is an urgent one. Leonora, will you go to your father—he is in his study—and tell him what we have arranged?' She turned back to the doctor. 'Perhaps while she is doing that you will advise me about this nasty little pain I get in my chest… My heart, you know…'

'I can hardly advise without a full examination; I suggest that you come down to the surgery one afternoon. I'm usually free then and you can tell me what is troubling you.' He added with brisk reassurance, 'You look extremely well.'

'Ah, but my looks have never pitied me,' said Lady Crosby in a resigned voice, 'and I don't complain.'

Leonora came back then, promised to be back in an hour or two and went out to the car with the doctor.

The drive to the surgery was so short that there was no need to talk and once they were there he set about explaining her work to her in a businesslike way which precluded any light-hearted chit-chat. She listened cheerfully, poked her nose into cupboards and drawers and asked intelligent questions.

'Like to start in the morning?' he wanted to know.

'Tomorrow? Well, why not? But you won't get too annoyed if I do everything wrong?'

'No, no.' He was laughing at her. 'I'm quite sure you will be able to cope well enough, and Mrs Crisp has promised that she will pop in just in case you need to know more about things. Half past eight, then?'

'All right. I'll ask Nanny if she knows of anyone who will come up to the house and help her. I could ask Mrs Pike too…'

'Good, that's settled. Now let us go and have our supper.'

Leonora said thoughtfully, 'There's no need, you know. I mean, you've explained everything to me here...'

He swept her out to the car. 'There's bound to be something I've forgotten,' he told her. 'I'll probably think of it during supper. There will be no time in the morning.'

A sensible observation to which she agreed. With pleasure and relief. She was hungry.

Cricket, accompanied by a boisterous Tod, admitted them, allowing his usual gloomy expression to be lightened with a smile at the sight of Leonora.

'Miss Crosby is having supper with me, Cricket,' said Dr Galbraith, and he took Leonora's jacket and ushered her across the hall and into the drawing room.

'Fifteen minutes, sir,' said Cricket, and melted away to the kitchen, where he set about adding one or two extra items the supper menu. He approved of Miss Crosby; it was a pity he hadn't been given more notice, for she was worthy of his culinary skill. He had already made baked pears, standing ready in their dish with the flavoured syrup poured over them, but he decided now to save them for tomorrow and prepare something else... There was also time to prepare a dish of anchoïades. With commendable speed he assembled anchovies, garlic, olive oil and lemon juice, sliced bread and black pepper. Cricket fetched his pestle and mortar and set to work.

In the drawing room the doctor invited Leonora to sit down, opened the door to allow Tod to join them from the garden and offered her a drink. Then he began a rambling conversation about nothing much. Apparently her job wasn't to be discussed for the moment. Leonora sipped dry sherry and allowed herself to enjoy the moment. Since she was hungry, she allowed her thoughts to dwell on supper.

She was not to be disappointed. Presently, sated at the elegantly laid table, she enjoyed the anchovies followed by quiche Lorraine, embellished by a potato salad, green peas and mushrooms tossed in garlic and cream. She ate everything, rather surprised by the lavishness of what she had supposed would be a simple meal.

Dr Galbraith was surprised too, amused that Cricket had found the time to add to what would have been a well-cooked meal but without fancy trimmings. He wondered what they would be invited to eat for pudding and hid a smile when Cricket served them with ice cream, tastefully decorated with burnt almonds, glacé cherries and chocolate shavings, the whole topped with whipped cream—a dessert Cricket was well aware that the doctor would have spurned. As it was, he ate his portion with evident enjoyment, offered Leonora a second glass of wine and suggested that they should return to the drawing room.

'I should really go home,' said Leonora, not wishing to go.

'I'll drive you back presently, but you must have some coffee first. Cricket makes very good coffee.'

'There must be something else I should know,' suggested Leonora. Supper had been delicious and so had the wine. The lovely room was restful and Dr Galbraith was a soothing companion.

The doctor, sitting in his chair on the other side of the fireplace, with Tod pressed against his knee, replied easily, 'Oh, I'm sure you have got a good grasp of what has to be done. You know most of the patients, I would suppose, which should make things easy for you.'

He drove her home soon after and bade her a cheerful goodnight, refusing her offer to come in to see her parents, getting back into his car with a friendly wave and driving away.

Her mother and father were in the drawing room and Leonora couldn't help but contrast its shabbiness with the well cared for comfort of Buntings. Perhaps, she reflected, she could find another job when she was no longer needed at the surgery and save enough money to have something done to the house. That it needed thousands of pounds spent on it she chose to ignore; just to do the urgent repairs and paint over the worst bits would at least stave off the ravages of time.

As she went in her mother said, 'Ah, there you are, dear. Everything is settled, I hope? Your father agrees with me that you did quite rightly to offer to help Dr Galbraith; it behoves us all to give help when it is asked for.'

'Yes, Mother,' said Leonora, and caught her father's eye. Lady Crosby was quite sincere but they both knew that she was the last person anyone would ask for help. Indeed, she was more than likely the one who needed it.

She arrived in good time at the surgery in the morning after a quick breakfast in the kitchen with Nanny, to find the doctor's car outside and, when she went in, the waiting room almost full.

There was no sign of the doctor, though. She wished everyone a good morning, took off her jacket and set to work getting out patients' notes. She hadn't quite finished when the surgery bell pinged and she put her head round the door to answer it.

'I'm nearly ready,' she assured him. 'Shall I give you those I have?'

He said placidly, 'Good morning, Leonora. Yes, please do. Let me have the others later. There is no hurry. I spend about seven minutes with each patient, sometimes more.'

He held out his hand for the notes. 'Who is first? Mrs Dodge? Send her in, will you?'

Leonora withdrew her head and then poked it back again. 'I forgot to say good morning,' she said, and closed the door.

Once she got over her initial uncertainty, she began to enjoy herself. She knew everyone there, which made things easy, for they were eager to point out everything she didn't do correctly.

Mrs Crisp always put the patients' notes on the little shelf by the desk when they had been seen by the doctor, old Mr Trubshaw told her, and when a small girl became restless several voices advised her that the WC was down the passage, and as the last patient went in she paused to tell her to put the kettle on. 'For the doctor's coffee,' she pointed out kindly.

With the waiting room empty, Leonora found mugs and coffee and while the kettle boiled began to tidy the place.

She felt pleased with herself; she hadn't done so badly. True, there had been one or two hitches but she hoped that the doctor hadn't noticed them. As the surgery door opened she turned off the gas and looked round at him, hopefully expecting a few words of praise.

She was to be disappointed. He walked to the door with barely a glance in her direction. 'I may be delayed. Could you ring Mrs Crisp and ask her if she'll come

here and take any calls? I'll do my best to get back by
evening surgery.'

He gave her a brisk nod and closed the door behind
him, so that she had no chance to say a word.

'Oh, well,' said Leonora, feeling deflated. 'Perhaps
he's late on his rounds.' She made herself a cup of coffee
and then phoned Mrs Crisp.

Mrs Crisp wasn't home. She had gone to Bath, her
husband said, and probably wouldn't be back until the
end of the week. Was there anything he could do?

Leonora said no, thank you and not to bother Mrs
Crisp when she got back, and sat down to think what
she should do. Obviously Dr Galbraith expected someone to be handy to take any calls or messages and he
wasn't to know that Mrs Crisp, who had volunteered to
come in in the afternoons, wasn't available.

'I can't leave here,' said Leonora, addressing the doctor's empty chair, and she picked up the phone again.
Nanny answered it, which was a good thing for she only
needed the barest explanation. 'I'll tell your ma. You've
nothing to eat there?'

'No, but there's plenty of tea and coffee and a little
milk.'

'Phone over to Mrs Pike and get her to make you a
sandwich; the boy will bring it over for you.'

When Leonora said there was no need, Nanny replied,
'You do as I say, Miss Leonora. Otherwise you'll be flat
on your back with hunger with the waiting room full of
patients this evening.'

As usual, Nanny was right; as lunchtime approached
Leonora's insides rumbled a reminder. She phoned Mrs
Pike and ten minutes later sank her splendid teeth into
the sandwiches that young Pike had brought over for her.
She devoured the lot, made a pot of tea and planned her

afternoon. If she had to sit there for several hours yet she might as well improve her mind and she had seen the books on the shelf in the surgery.

There had been several phone calls, none of them urgent, from patients wanting to make appointments, and it struck her suddenly that if the doctor was wanted urgently she had no idea where to find him.

'He should have told me,' said Leonora, talking to herself since there was no one else to talk to, and she went to see if there was a phone number she could ring. There was, tucked into the blotter on his desk, where, she supposed, if she had been trained for the job, she would have looked the moment he went out of the door. She was studying it when the phone rang.

Shirley Bates—Leonora recognised the voice at once. A cheerfully sluttish young woman living in one of the houses behind the main street. She had a brood of small children, a careless, easygoing husband and was known for her laziness.

'It's Miss Leonora, isn't it? My Cecil's that poorly. Nasty cough and 'e's covered in pimples. Measles or the like. The others 'ave 'ad it, but 'e didn't. 'E's very 'ot, won't eat or drink.'

'The doctor's out,' said Leonora, 'but I'll ask him to call and see Cecil as soon as he can. Could you put him to bed and give him plenty to drink and keep him warm?'

''E's in the kitchen watching telly, but I'll get 'im up to bed as soon as I've seen to the baby.' She sounded quite cheerful. 'Bye.'

Leonora wrote it all down and wondered if Cecil was someone the doctor would think urgent enough to be told about. Mrs Bates' children were a remarkably healthy brood despite their diet of potato crisps and fish and chips; on the other hand, Cecil, if she remembered rightly, was only five years old and measles could turn nasty if neglected.

She was weighing the pros and cons when the door opened and an old lady came in. Leonora knew her too. Old Mrs Squires, seventy-odd, widowed, and what her neighbours charitably called 'difficult'. She was comfortably off and lived alone in a small house in the main street and, having nothing better to do with her days, imagined herself to be suffering from various illnesses. She was also the local purveyor of gossip and Leonora greeted her warily.

'Mrs Squires—I'm afraid the doctor isn't here. Surgery is at five o'clock.'

'Well, of course I know that.' Mrs Squires seated herself in the waiting room. 'But I am feeling ill; he must be fetched here to see me. It's his duty.'

'He is out on a case,' said Leonora. 'I should go home and rest and come back at five o'clock.'

Mrs Squires shot her a cross look. 'I shall complain about your treatment, Miss Crosby—the Patient's Charter, you know.'

'But I haven't treated you, Mrs Squires. I really should go home if I were you. I'll see that you are first in at five o'clock.'

'Very well.' But the old lady didn't budge. 'You're not wearing your ring. I did hear...well, never mind that. Broken it off, have you? Such a charming man too. Let's hope you get another chance.'

'Oh, I expect I shall,' said Leonora cheerfully, hiding her doubts and unhappiness. 'Now if you don't mind I must ask you to go. I have to turn out this room before the evening surgery.'

Mrs Squires tittered. 'Fancy you dusting and sweeping. The young lady from the house. I wonder what that Mr Beamish of yours would say to that?'

Leonora held her tongue and ignored a desire to shake Mrs Squires until her false teeth rattled in her head. Instead, she held the door open and smiled.

Mrs Squires, despite her rudeness a little in awe of the Crosby family, left, tottering dramatically on the step and hoping *sotto voce* that Leonora wouldn't regret her unkindness when she, a poor widow, was found dead in her bed.

Leonora shut the door and locked it and the phone rang.

It was Mrs Bates again. 'My Cecil, 'e's been sick all over the carpet; 'e's real poorly and 'e don't talk much. Gone all pale and limp.'

'I'll try and get the doctor at once, Shirley. Is Cecil in his bed?'

''E didn't want ter go. 'E's still in the kitchen.'

'Keep him warm and get him to drink a little. I'm sure the doctor won't be long. I'll phone him now.'

Leonora dialled the number on the desk and when someone answered she said with relief, 'Oh, it's you, Mr Willis. Is Dr Galbraith there? May I speak to him? It's urgent.'

'I'll fetch him, Miss Leonora. He's on the point of leaving.'

'Well?' said the doctor in her ear.

'I'm glad I caught you,' said Leonora, relief making her voice sharp. 'Mrs Bates—the council houses—you know? Her Cecil's ill.'

She recited his symptoms in a voice which she strove to keep level. 'Will you go there? Thank heavens you aren't miles away...'

'Phone Mrs Bates and tell her I'm on my way. Why are you still at the surgery?'

'Because Mrs Crisp is in Bath, isn't she? Gone to see her mother.'

All she had in reply was a grunt before he hung up.

'Miserable man,' said Leonora, and put the kettle on and rang Mrs Bates once more. She would have a cup of tea; heaven knew, she deserved it after such a trying day. In an hour it would be surgery again and by the time she had tidied the place she would be just in time for dinner at home.

All the same, she reflected, putting a teabag in the pot, the day had gone quickly and she had had no time to think. A week or two like this, she thought ruefully, and Tony would seem like a dream—rather a bad one. But, good or bad, she had to get over it, hadn't she? And make a future for herself. While she'd been engaged to Tony, her head had been largely filled with plans for the future, the wedding, new clothes—she had expected to be happy ever after!

It was almost five o'clock and the waiting room was half-full when the doctor came in. Leonora had laid the case notes on his desk and, the moment he rang, ushered in Mrs Squires.

She was ushered out again within five minutes and Leonora wondered what he had told her to make her look so pleased with herself. Leonora sent in the next patient and wondered what the doctor had been doing all day. He hadn't said a word to her, had barely glanced at her as he'd gone to his surgery. He had told her that it was an easy job. Well, she thought rebelliously, let him find another slave to do his work. She had agreed to help out purely from kindness of heart; she didn't need the money...

A small voice reminded her that the money was going to be very useful. Provided she could persuade her father to accept it, it would allow the more urgent roof repairs to be made.

The last patient went away and she began tidying up magazines and setting chairs back in their places. She was on her knees collecting up the toys kept in one corner of the room for the benefit of the smaller patients when Dr Galbraith opened his door.

'Tell me what happened today…'

She recited the day's events in a rather cross voice. 'If you had taken the time to tell me what I was supposed to do,' she observed, 'or where you were going, or how long you would be away…'

She got up from the floor. 'Cecil? Is he very ill? Shirley Bates was so worried but I wasn't sure if you would consider him urgent.'

'I've sent him to Bristol. He has meningitis.'

She gulped in horror. 'Oh, heavens, should I have phoned you earlier? Or got an ambulance or something?'

'You acted exactly as you should have done.' His calm voice reassured her, 'I think that he has a very good chance of recovery. I am sorry that you have had such a hard time of it. You must be famished…'

'Well, yes, I am, but Mrs Pike sent over some sandwiches for me at lunchtime. Did you get something to eat?'

He looked faintly surprised. 'Er—Cricket will have something for me when I get home.'

'Is Mrs Willis ill? She's not been well since her daughter left home.'

The doctor sat astride a chair and leaned on its back. 'Her daughter is home. She had twins this morning.' He smiled. 'That is why I was in a hurry. I got there just in time.'

Leonora said slowly, 'Her parents love her very much... Is she all right? And the babies?'

'All very fit. Tell me, was Mrs Squires very trying?'

'Yes. She came in and sat down and said she was ill. I do hope she's not...' She gave him an anxious look. 'You see, I've known her for years and years and she has been ill with almost everything under the sun and no one believes her any more.' She frowned. 'I expect she's lonely but she's a gossip.'

'There is nothing wrong with Mrs Squires. And she is a gossip—a malicious one, I rather think. She told me that your callous treatment of her was on account of you being broken-hearted at the ending of your engagement.'

'She said that? The whole village will have heard it in twenty-four hours.'

'I think not. I appealed to her good nature.'

She said coldly, 'There was no need for you to do that.'

'To interfere? Have you heard from Beamish, Leonora?'

'No, of course not. And I don't want to talk about it.'

'Naturally not,' he agreed blandly. 'I hope that when you do you will address him in the icy tones you are using on me.'

He got up, ignoring her indignant breath. 'I'll take you home. Do you think you can face another day after this one?'

'Of course I can. I've enjoyed myself,' said Leonora, still frosty. 'Mrs Crisp will be away for a few days; I'll bring sandwiches with me tomorrow.'

'No need. I'll come for you when I've done the morning round and we can have lunch at Buntings. I'll have the phone with me and take any calls.'

'There is no need,' began Leonora. 'I don't mind in the least.' She added ingenuously, 'The day has gone so quickly there was no time to think.'

'Good. You are beginning to recover your pride and courage. Only I do beg of you that when you see Beamish you remember to hang onto both at all costs.'

'I have no intention of seeing Tony again.'

'One never knows what is around the corner,' said the doctor placidly. 'Now let me drive you home before they send a search party for you.'

He got out of the car to open her door when they reached the house.

'Thank you for holding the fort so sensibly, Leonora. Don't let your soft heart overrule your good sense when you see Beamish.'

'I'm not going to see him.'

He didn't answer her. Of course she would see him; he would even now be planning his visit, sure of its success. The doctor was very certain of that.

He was quite right.

# CHAPTER SEVEN

LEONORA'S second day at the surgery went smoothly. True, she wasn't very quick at finding the patients' notes in the filing cabinets but she was unfussed by the telephone and the appointments book.

The morning flashed by; she was surprised when the last patient went away and Dr Galbraith put his head round the door. 'How about coffee while I give you a list of where I'll be? If you need me and can't reach me from that, use the number on the desk—my own phone. When is Mrs Crisp coming home?'

'Mr Crisp thought at the end of the week.'

'Good. She'll take over here for the afternoons.'

He drank his coffee and drove away and she set about getting the notes out ready for the evening surgery. 'A man of few words,' she said, as usual talking to herself, and then wondered what he was really like when he wasn't being a doctor. She had had glimpses of that, but very briefly, and, for all she knew, his kindness and sympathy were all part of his being a doctor. Was he always calm and rather reserved? she wondered. Did he have a temper, get angry?

She washed the coffee-mugs and watered the potted plants on the waiting-room window-sill and after that there was a succession of phone calls—people wanting appointments, repeat prescriptions, a visit from the doctor—but there was nothing urgent and just before one o'clock he returned, popped her into the car and drove to Buntings.

Cricket was waiting for them, so was Tod, and they went briefly into the garden, going down to the end of it, throwing sticks for the dog and discussing bedding plants. It was a pretty garden, carefully tended but contriving to look as though everything growing in it had been there for ever and ever. Leonora stifled her envy. The garden at her house was twice as large and, despite her efforts, neglected.

Indoors again, they sat down to a cheese soufflé, salad, and a custard tart. They had their coffee at the table and Leonora, mindful of her duties, didn't linger over the meal.

'I must be getting back,' she said. 'Shall I ring you from the surgery so that you'll know I've taken the phone over again?'

'No—I'll drive you down. I want to see how Mrs Bates is coping. Cecil is going to be all right; she might like to visit him...'

'There isn't a bus until tomorrow.'

'I'm driving up to Bristol to see him. I'll take her with me.'

He's a kind man, reflected Leonora presently, watching him drive away from the surgery.

Another two days slipped by and Leonora now felt quite at home with the job. Indeed, she was vaguely regretful that Mrs Crisp would be home again tomorrow and would relieve her each afternoon, but despite the help Nanny had from Mrs Phelps from the village there was plenty to do when she was home, and her mother complained gently that while she was working the surgery took up so much time that it was impossible to have people to dinner; even an afternoon's bridge was difficult without Leonora being there to help with tea and make a fourth if needed.

'The bazaar, darling,' Lady Crosby had said with gentle reproach. 'Poor Lydia Dowling hasn't nearly enough helpers and you know what a great deal there is to do.'

Leonora had murmured a reply. Somehow, making pincushions and tray-cloths and sorting cast-off clothes for the jumble stall didn't seem important.

It was as the doctor was driving himself back from his morning rounds on Friday that he was passed on the road by a Porsche going too fast. Tony Beamish.

He glanced at his watch. Leonora would be back home by now; Mrs Crisp was always punctual and she had agreed to half past twelve as the time to take over for the afternoon. Any moment now Leonora would probably have to listen to Beamish's carefully planned explanations. Well, it was none of his business; she wasn't a child.

Later, as Cricket set his lunch before him, he gave a small, dry cough.

'Yes, Cricket?' Dr Galbraith was helping himself to ham but paused to look up.

'A message from Mrs Crisp, sir. She is unable to take over from Miss Crosby today. A migraine has laid her low.'

The doctor frowned. 'Miss Crosby is still at the surgery?'

'I presume so, sir. And Mrs Pike had occasion to telephone me a short time ago concerning your Bath Oliver biscuits which have arrived. Mr Pike was having a drink when Mr Beamish went to the pub. Very chirpy, she tells me, offered drinks all round and said he was on his way to see Miss Crosby. Unfortunately he was told that she was at the surgery.' Cricket paused to observe severely, 'It is regrettable how everyone knows everyone else's business in this village.' Then he resumed. 'Mr

Beamish drank his whisky, asked if he could leave his car at the pub and was seen walking to the surgery.'

The doctor was about to sample the ham, but he put down his knife and fork, got to his feet and whistled to Tod.

'I'll be back presently, Cricket. You had better set another place.' He smiled at Cricket. 'I'll just take a look.'

Mrs Crisp's phone call, just as Leonora was getting ready to hand over to her, was tiresome but since there was nothing to be done about it she would have to stay at the surgery. Dr Galbraith should be home about one o'clock; she would ring him and ask what she was to do.

She made a pot of tea, sat down at her table in the waiting room and began to sort out the patients' notes for the evening surgery, and at the same time allowed her thoughts to dwell on the pay packet she expected the next day. She was to be paid by the hour and she had worked quite a few hours extra during the week. Even after paying for Mrs Phelps there would be a useful sum. Perhaps she could get her father to have Mr Sims, the local builder, round to take a look at the roof.

She looked up as the door opened and Tony walked in.

At the sight of him she gave a little gasp, put down her mug of tea and put her suddenly shaking hands in her lap out of sight.

'Darling, you didn't think I'd let you go, did you? You see, here I am ready to go on my knees. I've no excuses, only that I was overwhelmingly busy when you came to see me and hardly knew what I was saying. Forgive me?' His smile was charming. 'Shall we start again? Just give me the chance to explain and you'll see how right I am. A marvellous future for us both—your parents will see what a splendid plan it is; it just needs a little persuasion from you—they listen to you, don't they?'

He came a little nearer, still smiling.

'Go away,' said Leonora. 'I'm working. Besides, I have no wish to speak to you ever again and I'll never forgive you—'

'Oh, come now, darling, you know you still love me.' His voice was beguiling.

'No, I don't. I can't bear the sight of you.'

He laughed then. 'Oh, you know you don't mean that.'

'Oh, but I do, and if you come a step nearer I'll throw this mug of tea at you.'

Tony laughed again, lunged forward and took the mug from her—just as the doctor came quietly through the door, tapped his elbow and sent hot tea pouring down his shirt and fashionable city suit. A few drops splashed his face too and he wiped them away furiously.

'You clumsy...'

He saw who it was then; he saw Tod too, standing by his master, all gleaming teeth and rumbling growls.

'Am I interrupting something?' asked the doctor genially. 'Is Mr Beamish annoying you, Leonora?'

She said, 'Yes. Please make him go away. I don't seem able to make him understand that I don't want to see or hear from him again.'

'Quite right,' agreed the doctor. 'Perhaps I should warn him that it might be as well if he did just that, for I don't like to see my friends harassed.'

He smiled at Tony, his eyes cold. 'I am a mild man, but if I get annoyed I can lose my temper. So be off with you, Beamish, and don't show your face here again

or there might be trouble. You had better take that suit
to the cleaners as soon as possible; tea stains are difficult
to remove.'

He stood aside and added gently, 'If you go quietly
Tod won't bite you.'

Tony went without a word, casting an apprehensive
eye at Tod, who leered at him.

The doctor shut the door after Tony had gone and
turned to look at Leonora. She was still sitting at the
desk, looking at the notes on it, determined not to cry.
She had been overjoyed to see the doctor but now she
felt humiliated too. He seemed to be everlastingly helping her out of awkward situations; he must consider her
a fool...

'Well, now that's dealt with,' said the doctor, 'we'll
go back and have our lunch.'

She still wouldn't look at him. 'Thank you for coming
when you did. It was lucky you did. Do you know that
Mrs Crisp can't come? I'll stay here—I've nothing much
to do at home this afternoon.'

'I'll take the calls on my phone; I'll drive you home
when we've eaten. I'm famished.'

'I'd rather not, if you don't mind.'

'I do mind. Where is your British phlegm, Leonora?'

'My phlegm? Oh...' She smiled then and looked at
him. 'Why do you always say the right thing, Dr
Galbraith?' She got up and picked up the mug from the
floor. 'I didn't know he was coming.' She gave the doctor a questioning look. 'Did you?'

He smiled at her. 'Not until Cricket told me. Cricket
always has his ear to the ground; he never misses a whisper of gossip or news and this is a small village. And
Beamish passed me in his car as I drove back.' He saw
her look. 'No, I didn't intend to interfere, Leonora. I

supposed that you would be home and he would have to deal with your parents as well as you, and it is hardly any of my business. But Cricket's information rather changed my plans.'

'Well, thank you very much. I expect he would have gone but I—I was glad when you came in with Tod.'

'Oh, Tod can put the fear of God into anyone,' said the doctor easily.

'I think you can too,' said Leonora.

She went with him then, back through the village and into Buntings, to find Cricket waiting, his sombre countenance breaking into a wintry smile at the sight of her. While they had been gone he had whisked up a feather-light cheese omelette, made a jug of lemonade, since he had decided that Miss Crosby wasn't a young lady to drink the doctor's beer, and prepared a little dish of chocolates to go with the coffee.

All of which Leonora enjoyed, almost her normal, matter-of-fact self once more. Only as they drank their coffee did she ask, 'You don't think he'll come back again?'

'No, I'm quite sure he won't.' The doctor handed her the dish. 'Have another of these chocolates. I don't know where Cricket gets them but they are quite good.'

Presently he drove her home. 'I'll have a word with your father if I may,' he told her as they got out of the car.

'Yes, of course. Don't leave Tod there; he likes Wilkins; they can go into the garden.'

As Tod joined them she said, 'We could go in through the garden door. I dare say Wilkins is somewhere in the garden at the back.'

He came to meet them and after a moment's wariness he lumbered off with Tod.

The garden door needed a coat of paint and its frame-work was by no means solid, and inside the house, going down the stone-floored passage towards the kitchen, the doctor saw the woeful state of the walls. He said nothing, of course, but Leonora said over her shoulder, 'We don't use this part of the house very much. It will be a great deal drier once we've had the roof repaired.'

'Old houses are difficult to maintain,' observed the doctor mildly, 'but it is surprising how well they last. Well built in the first place, of course.'

'Great-Great-Grandfather had it built,' said Leonora, and opened the door into the kitchen.

Nanny was sitting in her own particular chair by the Aga, knitting, and made to get up.

'No, don't move, Nanny,' said Leonora. 'We came in this way because of the dogs. I'm just taking Dr Galbraith to see Father.'

'You'll stay for tea?' said Nanny.

He refused with regret. 'I must go back and do some work—letters and so on. They do pile up. Another time if I may.'

'You're always welcome in this house,' said Nanny, 'and I speak for everyone in it.'

Leonora took the doctor to her father's study and then left them and went in search of her mother.

'Darling—you're late home. Have you been busy? The Dowlings phoned; Mrs Dowling wants you to go over when you can spare a minute—something to do with the jumble stall. I didn't hear you come in.'

'I brought Dr Galbraith through the garden door; he wanted to see Father.'

'I wonder why?' Lady Crosby put down the book she was reading and looked at Leonora. 'Is your father ill? No one told me.'

'No, no, nothing like that. Tony Beamish came to the surgery earlier; I think Dr Galbraith thought it better if he talked to Father about him.'

'Oh, dear. Was he horrid? But you weren't alone with him?'

'Only for a short while before Dr Galbraith came back to the surgery.'

'And...?' said Lady Crosby. 'Did he send Tony packing?'

'Yes,' said Leonora. She would have liked to tell her mother all about it but, much as she loved her parent, she was aware that anything unpleasant or worrying was ignored by her. She would tell Nanny presently and they would have a good laugh over it.

The two men came into the room a little later and her father said, 'I'm sorry that you have been bothered by young Beamish, my dear. I understand from Dr Galbraith that we are unlikely to see or hear from him again.' Sir William blew out his moustache and looked fierce. 'The scoundrel, wanting to turn us out of our home, pretending to be in love with Leonora. It must have been pretence; no man would behave in such a manner towards the girl he intended to marry.'

The doctor, watching Leonora, saw her blush and reflected that she should do that more often; it turned her pretty face into a thing of beauty. Even in her rather dull country clothes she was lovely. He had a sudden wish to see her decked out in haute couture and jewels—sapphires and pearls, he thought, long, dangling earrings and rings on her fingers. She had pretty hands...

'You must come to dinner one evening.' Lady Crosby's voice cut into his thoughts. 'We don't entertain much these days, but we are always glad to see our friends and neighbours.' She smiled up at him. 'Is Leonora proving satisfactory at the surgery?'

'Indeed she is, Lady Crosby. I'm thinking of asking her to stay on permanently—part-time, perhaps, sharing with Mrs Crisp when she returns.'

'Really? Well, why not? It is quite proper for us to help in the village in any way we can.'

The doctor didn't bat an eyelid. 'You are quite right, Lady Crosby; I am glad you agree with me.' He shook hands then, said a few words to Sir William, and added casually to Leonora, 'I'll see you around five o'clock,' and followed her out into the hall. At the door he whistled for Tod and got into his car, aware that Leonora was glowering at him from the steps.

He didn't drive away but opened his door and got out, leaning on the car roof, watching her come towards him.

'What's all this, then?' she wanted to know. 'Have I been asked if I want to go on working for you?' She added coldly, 'It's usual to be asked before it's talked about.'

He considered this muddled speech. 'I apologise; I was attacking you from the rear, wasn't I? But when you've cooled down, Leonora, consider the offer, will you? And let me know when you've made up your mind.'

He got back into the car and she stuck her head through the window.

'Of course I'll come permanently,' she told him. She sniffed. 'Since I've been asked...'

'Splendid.' He raised a hand and drove away. 'Now what possessed me to do that?' he enquired of Tod sitting beside him.

Tod didn't answer. Eyes half-shut, he was comfortably drowsy after a good romp in the garden with Wilkins.

Leonora went back into the house and found her father in his study.

'You like the idea of working for Dr Galbraith?' he asked her as she went in. 'It curtails your freedom...'

'Father, if I had all day with nothing to do—' and that's a joke, she reflected, thinking of the bed-making and hoovering and cooking, about which he was apparently unaware '—I would have to fill it with doing the flowers and helping Mrs Dowling with her bazaars and visiting. I really enjoy it.'

She hesitated. 'And Father, I get well paid and I don't need the money.' A fib, that! 'Could we have the roof over the kitchen mended? If I lent you the money? I really have no use for it, and if I put it in the bank it's just there doing nothing, whereas the tiles are falling off all the time.' She saw his frown. 'Please, Father...'

'The money is yours, my dear; you must wish to spend it on some new clothes—something for your mother, perhaps.'

'There's enough for that as well. It's too soon to buy clothes for the summer anyway, but I'll take Mother up to town later on and we'll shop. The roof first, though!' She smiled at him. 'Just between us two.'

'I do not care to take money from my daughter,' said Sir William.

'You're not; I'm lending it. It makes sense, you know, for if one or two repairs aren't made the house will fall apart and won't be of much use to me when I eventually get it.'

'There's that, of course. Very well, my dear, provided that you promise to spend your money on yourself once the roof is seen to. I'll get Sims to come round and inspect it. He might deal with it while this weather holds.'

She went to him then and kissed the top of his head. 'Don't tell Mother.'

Sir William allowed himself to smile. 'No, no, I won't. In any case your mother has very little idea about repairs and so forth.'

Leonora went to the door. 'I'm going to make scones for tea…'

'Yes, yes, of course, Leonora. I'm sorry about Tony Beamish. Your whole future.'

Leonora said matter-of-factly, 'Father, it would have been a disastrous one. I much prefer the future Dr Galbraith has offered me and living here in the village. I would have been unhappy in London and I'm sure that is where Tony and I would have lived for most of the time.'

Nanny, told of Leonora's job probably turning out to be a permanent one, was pleased. 'You'll see a bit of life even if it's only the folk living around here. And you'll have a bit of money to call your own.' She glanced at Leonora. 'You like working for the doctor? You like him as a person?'

'Yes, I do. I didn't think I was going to at first but he kind of grows on one, Nanny, and he was rather splendid when Tony turned up.'

'So you'll go every morning and evening?'

'Yes, but for the moment I'll go all day; Mrs Crisp isn't coming back for a couple of days. She had a bad migraine so she's taking a few days off, but when she starts she'll relieve me at half past twelve and stay until I go back at half past four. Of course, I'll be free on Saturday afternoons and Sunday.'

'Well, that's nice,' said Nanny cosily, and thought

how well the pair of them were suited. Perhaps if they saw more of each other... 'I'll make the tea if those scones are ready; it's almost time for you to go to the surgery.'

Dr Galbraith had nothing to say about Tony when she saw him that evening. There weren't many patients and when he had seen the last one he bade her goodnight, reminded her to lock up carefully and drove away. She watched him go, feeling vaguely disgruntled, although she reminded herself that she had no reason to be.

The doctor would be away for the weekend; she had been given a phone number to contact his stand-in at Wells and the phone had been switched through to him. 'I'll be taking over again early on Monday morning. Enjoy your weekend.' He had gone before she could reply.

Well, she would enjoy her weekend, she supposed. A long-delayed visit to the Dowlings to discuss the bazaar, her turn to do the flowers in church, and her mother had some friends coming to tea in the afternoon. Leonora felt restless. She wondered where the doctor was going—to see whoever it was who had called his dog Tod? He had made no secret of his affection for her, had he? I hope she's nice, reflected Leonora; he deserves a good wife.

She thought about him a good deal during the weekend, imagining him in a variety of situations—at the theatre, dining out with the unknown girl, meeting friends. In fact she thought about him so much that she quite forgot to think about Tony. He had disappeared out of mind as well as out of sight.

Leonora's imaginings were very wide of the mark. The doctor spent his weekend with his sister who lived with her farmer husband and three children in a lovely

old house on the outskirts of Napton on the Hill, a small
village in Warwickshire. Far from the theatre-going and
dining out that Leonora had envisaged, he walked and
rode and pottered around in old tweeds, ate huge meals
in the vast old-fashioned kitchen and kicked a football
around with his two small nephews. When he was tired
he sat down and his small niece climbed onto his lap
and demanded stories. She wanted to know about Tod
too.

'He's very well,' her uncle assured her. 'Though that's
a funny sort of name you gave him. A young lady I
know doesn't much like it.'

'What young lady?' his sister, who had just joined
them, wanted to know.

'A quite beautiful young lady with a great deal of dark
hair and a sharp tongue. Very sensible too.'

'Lives in the village?'

'Yes. I imagine her ancestors owned it at one time.
She lives in a lovely house that's mouldering away for
lack of money, with her mother and father.'

'And does good works?'

'Oh, yes.'

'Well, go on,' said his sister. 'Is she married, engaged,
and do you like her?'

'She was going to be married but luckily no longer,
neither is she engaged—not at the moment. Yes, I like
her. A series of—er—happenings made it possible for
me to ask her to be my receptionist at the surgery. She's
quite good—needs the money to have the roof repaired.'

'But if she's the daughter of the manor...' began his
sister.

'I used cunning; I implied that she would be undertaking vital charitable work.'

'You've been to a lot of trouble.'

The doctor sat back with his eyes closed. 'Funnily enough, until now I was unable to understand why.' He opened one eye. 'Is it time for tea?'

He was about to get into his car on Sunday evening when his brother-in-law said, 'Molly would like to come over and see you. Would that be all right?'

The doctor smiled. 'Jeffrey, Molly wants to get a look at my new receptionist. Of course you must all come—make it a Saturday if you can; on Sunday she is much taken up with church and Sunday lunch.'

He got into his car and Tod got in beside him. 'I'll do my best to arrange a meeting but it's quite likely that she will refuse to come. She isn't sure if she likes me. You see, I have been witness to some of her more delicate situations.' He laughed. 'Why, when we met for the first time she tripped up in the lane and sat down hard a few yards from the car. Very tart she was too, and then disarmed me completely by apologising for being rude. You'll like her.'

He thought about her as he drove back to Pont Magna. 'She is beginning to take up too many of my thoughts,' he told Tod, 'probably because I haven't met a girl like her before—and I'm not sure if I want that.'

He pulled one of Tod's silky ears gently. 'Ah, well, back to work in the morning and that will give me plenty to think about.'

So when Leonora arrived on Monday and poked her head round the surgery door to say good morning she was taken aback by his cool rejoinder and impersonal blandness.

He's quarrelled with her, she reflected, finding notes and marshalling the patients into seats. A full house too—nasty coughs, a black eye, a toddler with suspicious spots and the snuffles, and the verger, who had fallen down the last few steps of the narrow, winding stairs to the church tower and had got some nasty bruises as a result.

The doctor didn't wait for his coffee after surgery. 'You've got the phone number,' he reminded her. 'I'll call in when I get back. You had better come back to my place for lunch.'

'I've brought sandwiches, thank you.' She spoke in a cool voice; if he wanted to be frosty she would be too. 'There are a lot of patients for the evening clinic. If any more phone…?'

He took a quick look at the appointments book. 'I'll see two more—anyone else, unless it's urgent, must come in the morning. That's pretty full too—and young Beamish told me it was an easy job!'

He watched the colour creep into Leonora's cheeks. Did she still love the man? Surely not… His frown was so ferocious that she looked at him in astonishment but he had gone before she could say anything.

She spent the next hour or so tidying the place—cleaning bowls and the simple instruments he had used, cleaning up the magazines and toys—and finally put on the kettle for a cup of coffee to go with her sandwiches. There had been several phone calls for appointments and she had got out the notes for the evening surgery.

She made the coffee and bit into the first of Nanny's cheese sandwiches. The phone rang and she swallowed hastily and said, 'Hello, Dr Galbraith's surgery,' in a rather thick voice.

It was a call from Willis Farm. 'It's the baby—'e don't look well; the doctor must come 'fore 'e gets any worse.'

Leonora picked up the pen. 'It's Janice, isn't it? Which baby is it? You had a boy and a girl, didn't you?'

'Never you mind; just send the doctor.'

'He isn't here, but I can get him for you, only I must know what to tell him. Now, which baby?'

'The boy—we calls 'im Billy. Looks kind of poorly and keeps screaming.'

'The little girl's all right?'

'Yes, far as I can see. Where is 'e, then?'

'I can phone him at once. Isn't your mother there?'

'Ain't no one 'ere. Ma's gone ter Radstock Market and the men are down the ten-acre field.'

'Go back to the babies, Janice,' said Leonora. 'I'm going to phone the doctor now; he'll come just as soon as he can.'

She was putting the phone down when he walked in.

'That was Janice,' said Leonora. 'She says one of the twins is ill and she's alone—the men are at the other end of the farm, and her mother's in Radstock.'

'Did she tell you what was wrong?'

'Only that Billy looked poorly and screamed a lot.'

He went to his locked cupboard in the surgery and selected the items he wanted, put them in his bag and said, 'Right, then, we'd better go.'

We? She couldn't help casting a look at the sandwiches, but since he didn't respond she followed him out of the door, which he locked before opening the car door and urging her in.

He didn't appear to be hurrying but he hadn't wasted a moment. As they left the village street she asked, 'Why must I come with you? I don't know anything much about babies.'

He turned to look at her. 'No, no—you are coming as my chaperon.'

'Chap...' For a moment she was speechless. 'Whatever for?'

'Have you seen Janice since she came back from London?' he asked.

'No. She was a quiet girl—not very friendly with anyone else here, quite pretty, though—she had nice mousy hair...'

She gave him an enquiring look which he ignored, and he didn't speak again until he'd driven into the farmyard, got out, opened her door and fetched his bag from the back seat. A girl was standing at the open door watching them. If this was Janice, where was the mousy hair, the pretty face? This girl had shorn locks of a vibrant chestnut colour and so much make-up that it was hard to tell what she really looked like. She had a stud in one nostril, long, dangling earrings and the shortest skirt Leonora had ever seen.

'Where's this baby?' asked the doctor in a voice nicely compounded of professional reserve and kindness. 'Tell me exactly when he became ill. Is he feverish? Being sick?'

He went past her into the house, saying over his shoulder, 'Leonora, come with me, please.'

Janice led the way upstairs to where the babies were lying in their cots. The baby girl was sleeping but Billy was roaring his head off, red in the face, waving minute fists in rage. The doctor picked him up.

'He's sopping wet,' he observed mildly. 'Get some dry clothes for him—he needs changing for a start.'

Janice went to a chest of drawers and started rummaging in it and he handed the baby to Leonora, who rightly deduced that she was meant to undress the infant. She laid him gently in his cot again and took off his old-fashioned gown and the wringing wet nappy and exposed a small sore bottom.

'He needs a bath,' she said, and added, 'Sorry...'

'You haven't bathed the babies today,' stated the doctor. 'And when were they last changed? Billy isn't ill; he's wet and very sore. Get a bath ready for them; let's get both of them washed and then I'll examine them and make sure there is nothing wrong. When did the district nurse come?'

'Yesterday. Don't want 'er, old Nosy Parker; told 'er she didn't need ter come any more.'

'Your mother knows this?'

'Ma don't know nothing.' She shrugged her shoulders and went out and presently came back with a small bath and then warm water.

The baby girl—Daisy—was awake now; Leonora, without being asked, stripped the cots while the babies were being bathed, made them up again with clean sheets and then sat down with a towel on her lap so that Billy could lie on it while his poor sore bottom was examined by the doctor.

Leonora held him gently, stroking the fair hair on his small head, telling him what a good boy he was, all the while aware of the doctor's face within inches of her own as he bent down, and aware too of a peculiar feeling somewhere under her ribs which resolved itself into a flood of happiness. Not that she had the leisure to think about it. Billy was wriggling like a very small eel and crying again.

'When did they have their last feed?' asked the doctor.

'Oh, I dunno—this morning. Ma went early; she fed 'em.'

'Go and get their feed now. There is nothing wrong with either of your babies. They were hungry, dirty and wet. Tell me, would you like them to go to the children's hospital for a few weeks while you decide what you intend to do?'

'Yeah, that's a good idea. What am I supposed to do with two kids anyway? Didn't want 'em, did I?'

'They could be adopted.'

'That suits me fine.' She flounced away to fetch the babies' bottles and the doctor got out his phone while Leonora tucked Daisy in her cot once more. Billy began to bawl again, so she picked him up and cuddled him, listening vaguely to the doctor's voice. He was on the phone for a long time.

She accepted a bottle from Janice and began to feed Billy; he gulped and choked in his haste and she wondered if he had been getting as much as he needed. The doctor must have had the same idea for he phoned again and then said, 'The district nurse is coming this afternoon; she will make up the babies' feeds for the rest of the day and make sure that they are all right. You will do exactly what she says, and as soon as it can be arranged Billy and Daisy will be taken to the hospital. I'll come and see your parents this evening.'

He glanced at Leonora. 'Ready to go? Nurse will be here within the next hour; she knows what to do.'

On the way back Leonora burst out, 'How could she? Such little babies and no one to love them—and that's all they want—food and warmth and love, isn't it?' She hadn't meant to weep but two tears escaped and ran down her cheeks.

The doctor, looking straight ahead, none the less saw them. He dropped a large hand on her arm for a moment. 'They will be adopted by people who will love them and care for them. I'll have to speak to her parents, of course, but I suspect that once she is free of the twins she will leave home again. In the meantime the district nurse will keep an eye on them and with luck we should get them transferred to hospital tomorrow or the next day.'

'It must be so satisfying to get things done,' said Leonora fiercely, 'to know what to do and to be able to get on with it.'

His reassuring grunt was comforting.

He glanced at his watch. 'It's three o'clock; at least no one has called on the phone. We'll get something to eat before we do anything else.'

'My sandwiches…' began Leonora.

'They'll be curling at the edges by now. Cricket will find us something.'

This was getting to be a habit, reflected Leonora—something which for some reason she found unsettling. 'If you don't mind I'll go straight to the surgery, Doctor.'

'I do mind—and call me James.' He didn't look at her but went on with casual friendliness, 'We are colleagues, are we not?'

'Well, yes, I suppose so,' she said doubtfully. 'You don't mind?'

His mouth twitched. 'Not at all. I should prefer it since we are to see a good deal of each other for the time being.'

Did that mean, she wondered worriedly, that he was already looking for another receptionist—a trained one who knew the difference between indigestion and a heart attack and who knew how to fend off those who came to the surgery apparently for the fun of it?

She said soberly, 'Very well, James.' After which it hardly seemed appropriate to mention the surgery again. Besides, she was hungry.

# CHAPTER EIGHT

MRS CRISP came back in a day or two—and perhaps that was as well, thought Leonora. Working for the doctor in the surgery was one thing, but somehow lunching with him in his lovely house with Cricket beaming at her—and feeling so happy while she was there—was unsettling.

She was careful to work the hours he had suggested and made no effort to talk to him unless it was about a patient or phone call. He didn't seem to mind, she reflected forlornly. True, he had stopped one morning to tell her that Billy and Daisy were in hospital and thriving and their mother had packed her bag and left home again.

'How can you possibly leave two little babies?' Leonora had wanted to know.

He had smiled thinly and shaken his head and gone away again to see to his patients.

She was handing over to Mrs Crisp on her first afternoon back when he came into the surgery, wished Mrs Crisp a good day and then said, 'Leonora, my sister is coming down on Saturday for the weekend. I'd like you to come to tea.'

If they had been alone she would have made some excuse—not that she didn't want to accept, but she had decided, hadn't she, that she would take care not to get too friendly. She wasn't very clear why this was necessary but that was beside the point. Mrs Crisp, standing there smiling and nodding, made it difficult to refuse. Besides, he didn't give her a chance to do so.

'Around three o'clock,' he said easily. 'We look forward to seeing you.'

When he'd gone Mrs Crisp observed chattily, 'I wonder who else will be there?'

Leonora felt a pang of relief and then disappointment; there would be half the village there, no doubt. She reminded herself that that was exactly what she wanted.

Lady Crosby puckered her brows when Leonora told her that she would be going to Buntings for tea. 'Strange that Dr Galbraith didn't include your father and me. Will there be many there, I wonder?'

'I've no idea. He mentioned his sister staying with him—she has three small children, Mrs Crisp tells me.'

'In that case I would have refused. With children there can be no conversation. I dare say there will be another dinner party shortly. You haven't met any of his friends?'

'Mother, I'm at the surgery; even if he had friends staying they wouldn't come there.' Was now the time to mention the lunches she had had at Buntings? she wondered, and decided against saying anything. Her mother would jump to the conclusion that Dr Galbraith—she must remember to call him James—was interested in her. Which he wasn't. Even when he had invited her to tea he had sounded exactly like the family doctor talking to a patient.

On Saturday, uncertain as to who might be there, she got into her jersey dress and a long cardigan, both in a pleasant shade of turquoise-blue and both in a style guaranteed to be wearable five years hence, arranged her hair in a chignon, made up nicely, thanking heaven that it was a dry, quite warm day so that she could wear light shoes. She had considered biking there but then she might arrive a bit tousled. She bade her parents goodbye, told Nanny she would be back around six o'clock, perhaps earlier, and walked to Buntings.

Walking up the drive to the house, she gave a small sigh of envy. It looked charming; the flowerbeds were full of spring flowers now, and the shrubbery was newly green. The door was open and as she reached it two small boys darted out.

They came to a halt by her and offered grubby hands. 'You are Leonora,' said the taller of the two. 'I'm Paul; he's George.'

Leonora shook hands. 'Hello, Paul; hello, George. How did you know who I was?'

'Uncle James told us. Come inside.'

The doctor came to meet them as they entered the hall. His greeting was casual and friendly. 'The house is in an uproar; I hope you don't mind. Come and meet Molly and my brother-in-law. There's another child somewhere—my niece.'

They all went into the drawing room and she shook hands with Molly and Jeffrey and then stooped to take the little girl's hand. 'I'm two,' she whispered, and buried her face in her mother's skirt. Presently she peeped up at Leonora. 'Uncle James and me share Tod.'

'Now, that's nice,' said Leonora, bending down. 'I've got a dog too. His name's Wilkins.'

A small hand was slipped into hers. 'I'll show you Tod.'

They all went into the garden then, and the talk was easy and pleasant and made her feel perfectly at home. Tod was admired, stroked and offered a ball while they strolled around, the children darting to and fro, the grown-ups stopping to discuss some plant or other.

Molly tucked an arm into Leonora's, not asking questions, mentioning only casually Leonora's work at the surgery, but telling her about the children and her life on the farm.

'I don't do any farm work—I wouldn't know how to and Jeffrey has an agent—but it's a nice old house and there's heaps of room for the children. We ride too—do you?'

'I used to.' Something in Leonora's voice caused Molly to start an animated conversation about her children. 'They're a handful even with Nanny's help. Of course, they're as good as gold when they come down here. They adore James; he makes a marvellous uncle and, heaven knows, he has enough practice—we have four sisters, did you know? Two of them are married with children. They live a good way away, though— Scotland and the depths of Cornwall. The other two are in Canada with our father and mother—twins, waiting to go to university; they're the youngest.'

'It must be lovely to have a brother and sisters...'

'Oh, it is. We all like each other too. Here's Cricket to tell us tea is ready.'

It was a hilarious meal, sitting round the dining-room table with the children, and Cricket had done them proud. Tiny sandwiches, a plate of bread and butter cut paper-thin, fairy cakes, gingerbread men and a magnificent chocolate cake.

There was even a high chair for the little girl and when Molly saw Leonora looking at it she said, 'James keeps one here; there's always a baby or a toddler; as fast as one is big enough to sit on a chair there's another one ready for the high chair!' She laughed. 'Mother and Father say they lose count of their grandchildren.'

It wasn't quite what Leonora had expected but she

found herself wishing that she had a large family like the doctor's; their warmth and pleasure in each other's company was something she had never experienced and wasn't likely to. She didn't waste time repining, though. She ate a splendid tea, unaware of the doctor's eyes upon her, wholly taken up with the small boys sitting on either side of her.

After tea they played hide-and-seek round the house. As she raced round the passages, up and down the staircase, in and out of the rooms, Leonora's cheeks got flushed and her hair escaped in little curls; she was happy and a little excited, so that she looked prettier than ever.

Creeping up the back stairs, looking for a likely hiding place, she came face to face with the doctor.

They were at the end of a narrow passage leading to the back of the house, with doors on one side and a row of small windows overlooking the garden.

They stood looking at each other for a moment. 'Enjoying yourself, Leonora?' he asked, and smiled.

'Oh, yes—yes, I am. I'd forgotten what fun it was. We must hide…'

'We aren't really built for it, are we?' he observed. 'Rather on the big side.'

'Well, really!' began Leonora, suddenly aware of her magnificent proportions compared with Molly, who was a slender size eight. Her childish pleasure was pricked like a balloon. 'You're very rude,' she said tartly, and edged past him.

He put out a hand and stopped her very gently. 'I'm so sorry; would it make things better if I told you that I like my women big?'

He bent and kissed her quickly. 'Run along and hide. There's a large cupboard at the end of this passage.'

She wanted to run out of his house, get away from him, but she couldn't do that; she got into the cupboard and presently was discovered by a small boy shouting in triumph.

It was the children's bedtime then. Leonora was embraced in turn, shook hands with Molly and Jeffrey, thanked the doctor in a chilly voice for a pleasant afternoon, took her cardigan from Cricket and went to the door.

She found the doctor beside her. 'I'll walk with you,' he told her affably. 'The house will be bedlam until the children are in bed.'

Short of turning and running for it there was nothing she could do about it, not with Cricket watching. She said nothing at all in a rather marked manner, told Cricket what a delightful tea he had given them, and walked out of the door, stiff with dignity.

'Why are you cross?' asked the doctor blandly, strolling along beside her. 'Is it because I called you a big girl or because I kissed you?'

'Both,' snapped Leonora. 'And I would much prefer to walk home alone.'

He ignored this. 'But you are a big girl,' he pointed out in a reasonable voice. 'But, I must add, most splendidly shaped; to say otherwise would be an outrage.'

'You shouldn't talk to me like this,' said Leonora, marching along, very red in the face.

'Should I not have kissed you either? I enjoyed it.'

So did I, thought Leonora, although she wasn't going to say so. She kept a haughty silence and saw Mrs Pike peering at them from the closed door of her shop, which prompted her to say in a peevish voice, 'There is absolutely no need to walk home with me.'

He stopped and turned her round to face him. 'I do

not know what has made you so contrary. We are colleagues, are we not? And I thought we were friends.' He
grinned down at her. 'And I wonder what Mrs Pike
thinks we are?'

'Is she still peeping? Oh, please, Dr Galbraith, may
we walk on?'

'Call me James...'

'James,' she went on, 'you're impossible...'

She stopped. He wasn't impossible; he was James
who laughed at her because she was a big girl and was
silly about being kissed, and she wished she had never
met him. She wished too that she didn't love him. Why
would she discover that in the middle of the village's
main street with curtains twitching right and left of
them?

They were walking on, side by side, not touching. She
felt quite dizzy with the sudden discovery of her love.
This was love, she realised; whatever she had felt for
Tony hadn't been that—more of an infatuation, she supposed. She wanted to tell James, which was absurd; instead, anxious to break the silence between them, she
started to talk about the children.

He answered her with casual good nature and it
amazed her that he couldn't know how she felt. But why
should he?

At the house, he stayed for a short time, talking to her
mother and father, then he bade her a brisk goodbye and
strode off home, turning to wave at the open gate.

'Who else was there?' her mother wanted to know.
'He has many friends, I'm sure.'

'Well, there was his sister and brother-in-law and their
three children.'

'No one else? How extraordinary. Was it boring, darling?'

'No. We played hide-and-seek all over the house—the children are charming.' Leonora smiled to herself. 'We had tea round the table in the dining room—with the children...'

'Surely there was a nanny?'

'Oh, yes. She was having the afternoon off.'

Lady Crosby picked up her book. 'Well, as long as you weren't bored, Leonora. It sounds to me like the waste of an afternoon—you would have enjoyed yourself more if you had gone to the Dowlings'. Their niece is staying—such a pretty girl; plenty of money, I hear; I'm surprised Dr Galbraith wasn't invited.'

Leonora felt an instant hatred for the niece. She said abruptly, 'I'll go and see if Nanny needs any help with dinner,' and took herself off to the kitchen, where she got in Nanny's way until she was told to take Wilkins for a walk. 'For I don't know what's got into you, Miss Leonora,' said Nanny. 'Proper crotchety you are and no mistake.'

So she took Wilkins out into the garden and then into the park, and since there was no one else to tell she told him all about James.

'I can quite see,' she told him, 'that it's being an only child. I mean I can't talk to Mother and Father, if you see what I mean—talk to them like they were all talking together at James's house, saying what they really meant and knowing that the others were listening...'

Wilkins pressed up against her, staring up into her face with soft brown eyes; he was her friend and offering sympathy, and Leonora, who almost never cried, cried a little now and felt better. 'I'll see him on Monday,' she said, and blew her pretty nose and went back indoors and laid the table for Nanny.

She woke several times during the night, thinking

about James, longing to see him and at the same time dreading their meeting. She would have to behave as though nothing had changed and she wasn't sure if she would be able to manage that. To give up her job at the surgery would be the easiest way out of her dilemma; on the other hand, if she did that she wouldn't see him. Besides, Sims was going to start on the roof on Monday morning and would expect to be paid. She slept at length and woke with a heavy head.

Monday wasn't as bad as she had expected. For one thing the surgery was full and when the doctor came in there was no time for more than a brief good morning, and, for another, when he had dealt with his patients he went away at once, not waiting for his usual cup of coffee. He wasn't back when Mrs Crisp arrived and Leonora took herself off home.

If I can get through one day like that, I can get through the rest of them—until he finds a receptionist to suit him, she thought. She had calculated that Mr Sims would take three weeks to patch the roof; once that was done, if she didn't want to go on working for James she could think up some excuse and leave. After all, she had only gone to fill a gap, hadn't she? She refused to think further than that; a future without the doctor wasn't to be contemplated...

She managed very nicely during the next two weeks, offering him chilly good mornings and good evenings, making sure that there was never a chance for them to be alone. It took all her ingenuity at times, and the doctor, puzzled and a little amused, wondered what she was up to.

He played along with her; he was kind and friendly and impassive. He knew by now that he loved her and intended to marry her but he was content to await events.

Something was worrying his Leonora and, being a man without conceit, he was quite unaware of the truth.

The roof repaired, Mr Sims took away his ladders and Leonora's cheque, and since there was no further excuse to make as to why she had to continue working Leonora sought for a way of ending a situation which from her point of view was becoming increasingly awkward. Only the day before, James had suggested that she might like to have lunch with him at Buntings so that she could admire the garden. Her refusal had been so instant that he had lifted an eyebrow, watching her red face and listening to her trying to soften her sharp reply.

'That is, thank you very much, but I said I'd be home as soon as possible; I've several things to see to.'

He had smiled then and said placidly, 'Of course—another time.' Then he'd begun to talk about one of his patients who wanted to alter his appointment.

It wouldn't do—she would have to think of something.

As it turned out, she had no need to do that.

It was the following day, when she got home in time for lunch, that she found Nanny sitting in the kitchen looking flushed, and coughing a nasty little dry cough.

'You've caught cold,' said Leonora, and bustled her off to bed with a hot-water bottle and a hot drink and some aspirin. 'You stay there, Nanny—I'll see to the lunch and tea, and get supper when I get back this evening. Don't you dare get out of bed.'

'I'll feel better presently,' said Nanny, and fell into an uneasy doze.

Lady Crosby, informed of Nanny's poorly state, made a little face.

'Oh, dear, poor Nanny. Do you suppose it's flu? I'd better not go near her; you know how easily I catch things. I expect you can manage, darling. We can have an easy meal this evening—something you can deal with when you get back from the surgery. I don't suppose we need to send for Dr Galbraith.'

'Well, if Nanny's not better tomorrow I think you had better, Mother.'

'Of course if Nanny's ill she must be looked after. You'll see him this evening, won't you? Or tomorrow morning? I dare say it's just a feverish cold. Nanny is never ill.'

Leonora got the lunch, tidied up, took a look at Nanny and found her sleeping, and went to get the tea-tray ready and then examine the contents of the fridge. It would have to be a corned beef pie, disguised in a handsome dish. There were vegetables enough and some prawns in the freezer—prawn cocktails, she decided, the pie with a variety of vegetables and an egg custard. She could make a sauce from strawberry jam when she got home that evening.

She made Nanny a jug of lemonade before she left, turned her pillows and bathed her hot face and asked her mother to take a look from time to time. 'You don't need to go into Nanny's room—if you'd just take a look to make sure she's all right.'

'Very well, dear, since there is no one else. Supposing Nanny wants something or feels worse?'

'I'm sure you can cope, Mother, and I'll be back in a couple of hours.'

Lady Crosby looked vexed. 'To think that you should have been marrying Tony and looking forward to a settled future...'

Leonora thought of several answers to that but none of them seemed suitable.

There was only a handful of patients at the surgery

and Leonora glanced with relief at the clock as she started tidying up.

The doctor saw that. 'Going out this evening?' he asked casually.

'No. Oh, no. Nanny's got a bad cold so I said I'd get dinner this evening. She's keeping warm in bed.'

He was at his desk, locking the drawers, putting papers in his case.

'Not often ill, is she? A vigorous little lady.'

'She's a darling,' said Leonora warmly. 'I don't know how we would manage without her.'

'No—well, don't hang around. I'll lock up and see you in the morning. Let me know if you are worried about her and I'll take a look.'

'Yes, thank you, I will.'

She hurried home and found her mother playing patience in the drawing room while her father read.

'How's Nanny?' she asked.

Her mother looked up. 'Hello, darling. I peeped in once or twice; she seemed quite comfortable—coughing a bit, but what does one expect with a heavy cold?' She turned over a card. 'Are you going to be a clever girl and cook our dinner?' She smiled sweetly at Leonora. 'Something nice?' she added coaxingly.

'I'll surprise you,' said Leonora, and sped away, not to the kitchen but to Nanny's room.

Nanny was awake, hot and restless and thirsty. 'Your ma popped in but I didn't like to bother her,' she said when Leonora frowned at the empty jug.

'I'm going to wash your hands and face and put you into a fresh nightie and make your bed,' said Leonora. 'Then I'll bring you some soup and after that a cup of tea and some more aspirin.' She picked up the jug. 'Give me five minutes, Nanny.'

She whisked herself into the kitchen, popped the prepared pie in the oven, put the vegetables on the slow
burner and set the soup to warm. There was still a lemon;
she made a jug of lemonade, lavishly iced, and bore it
back to Nanny's room before gently washing her, sitting
her in a chair while she made the bed and fetched more
pillows. Then she settled her against them, a shawl
around her shoulders.

'That's better,' said Nanny. 'I do believe I'd like some
of that soup.'

The dinner was cooking itself, thank heaven. Leonora
took the soup upstairs and before Nanny started on it
took her temperature. It was up—not frighteningly so,
but none the less higher than it should be.

In the morning, she decided, she would ask James to
come and see Nanny—perhaps an antibiotic...? At the
moment Nanny seemed easier and when Leonora slipped
up to look at her just before she dished up she was
asleep.

She reassured her mother at dinner. 'Nanny's asleep
at present; if she has a quiet night I dare say her temperature will be down in the morning.'

'We can't have Nanny ill,' observed her father. 'Perhaps we should get Dr Galbraith to look in tomorrow
some-time.' He glanced at Leonora. 'You can manage,
my dear. I dare say we can get extra help...'

He looked around vaguely as if to conjure domestic
help out of the walls and Leonora said quickly, 'No
need, Father, I can manage.'

And her mother said, 'Of course you can, darling, and
I'll help.'

Leonora thanked her gravely, both she and her father
aware that Lady Crosby had no intention of altering her
gentle day's routine. She had always had a sheltered life,

first as a girl with doting parents and then as a wife cherished by a husband who shrugged off her inability to cope with domestic problems.

At first that hadn't mattered, for there had been money enough to employ a housekeeper and help in the house, and now, since he had lost most of his money, it was too late to change her ways. Leonora knew that too and accepted it. All the same, if Nanny were to be ill for more than a day or two it would be difficult to manage even with the help she had from the village.

She was a sensible girl; she decided to worry about that if and when it happened, and after a last peep at Nanny went to bed.

It was just after three o'clock when she woke, and a vague feeling of uneasiness got her out of bed, to creep out of her room and along the wide corridor leading to the passage where Nanny had her room.

Nanny was muttering and mumbling to herself, half choking on a nasty little cough, and she felt hotter than ever.

'Nanny,' said Leonora, 'how do you feel? Shall I get you a drink and bathe your face—cool you down a bit?'

Nanny didn't seem to hear, looking past her at the empty room, whispering to someone she couldn't see. Leonora turned the bedside lamp so that the light shone on Nanny. Her face was grey and somehow grown small and her breathing was harsh and quick.

Leonora flew through the house and down the staircase and picked up the phone. At the sound of the doctor's quiet voice she let out a great sigh of thankfulness.

'James, it's Nanny. She's ill—hot and restless and her breathing's funny—and she doesn't know me.'

'Unlock the front door and go back to her.' His matter-of-fact manner steadied her. 'I'll be with you in ten minutes.'

It was less than that when he came quietly into the room. He was wearing a thick sweater and trousers, his hair stood on end and there was a faint stubble on his chin, but his manner was as cool and self-assured as though he were in his surgery.

He took one look at Leonora. 'Go and put on a dressing gown before you catch cold; we may be here for a little while.'

His tone was impersonal but she flushed a little, until that moment forgetful of the fact that she had rushed to Nanny in a cotton nightie and bare feet. She nodded and disappeared silently, to reappear moments later, her dressing gown fastened tightly around her, slippers on her feet.

The doctor was bending over Nanny, going over her chest with his stethoscope. Presently he stood up. 'Pneumonia. I'll give her an injection—an antibiotic—and see if I can find her a bed. She needs hospital treatment.'

Leonora's eyes looked enormous in her pale face. 'She'll hate that...'

His voice was very gentle. 'At the moment she isn't very aware of where she is—she'll only need to stay for a few days until the antibiotics do their work, then we can have her back.'

He took his phone from his pocket and dialled and Leonora stood as quiet as a mouse, holding Nanny's hand, listening to his calm voice.

'There's a bed at Bath; I'll get an ambulance; the sooner she gets there the better.' He glanced at her. 'Get a bag and pack a few things, will you?'

'Yes. May I go with her? Please...'

'I'll take you in the car; I'll see her safely in bed and

bring you back here—hopefully in time for morning surgery.'

She nodded. 'I'll go and dress and get Nanny's things
together. Will you be all right here?'

He checked a smile and assured her gravely that he
would be.

She tore into the first clothes she laid hands on,
washed her face, dragged a comb through her hair and
tied it back with a bit of ribbon, before going back to
pack a bag for Nanny. An easy task. Nanny's drawers
were immaculate, garments folded exactly, beautifully
ironed, smelling of lavender bags. Leonora packed her
old-fashioned nighties, her dressing gown and slippers
and brush and comb and bag of toiletries, added her
spectacles and the Bible she kept on her bedside table
and closed the case.

The doctor was sitting on the edge of the bed, watching Nanny, completely relaxed. 'Shall I make a cup of
tea?' she asked. 'I got you out of bed very early…'

'A splendid idea, and bring a pencil and paper with
you. You must leave a note for your mother and father.
You don't want to wake them?'

'They would worry. Perhaps I could phone them from
the hospital.'

'A good idea. The ambulance should be here in fifteen
minutes or so.'

She crept down to the kitchen and made tea. Wilkins,
from his basket by the Aga, was pleased to see her,
accepted a biscuit and went back to sleep, and she went
back upstairs with two mugs and more biscuits on a tray.

While they ate and drank she composed a note and
showed it to the doctor. 'Would that do? I don't want
to upset them.'

He gave her a thoughtful look, read the note and

handed it back. 'That's fine. If you've finished your tea, we'll get Nanny wrapped up ready for the ambulancemen. They may wake your parents…'

'Probably not; their room is at the back of the house and there's a door to the passage leading to it. Shall I creep in and leave the note? And then if they're awake I can tell them.'

He nodded without speaking and began to wrap Nanny carefully in a blanket. She was quieter now, unaware that she was coughing.

Leonora whispered, 'Is she very ill?' She added sharply, 'Tell me the truth.'

'Yes, but I hope that we have caught it in time. She's a tough little lady.' He listened. 'There's the ambulance. Go and let them in; tell them to be quiet.'

When they came into the room, he told her to go to her parents' room with the note and then go down to the hall. 'And bring a jacket.'

Her parents didn't stir as she opened their door, put the note on a bedside table and crept out again, closing the door after her. The men were loading the stretcher into the ambulance as she reached the hall and as they shut its doors the doctor went to his car. 'Jump in—I'll close your front door.'

She got in and sat silently while he drove, keeping the ambulance in sight. It was beginning to get light now and she felt a strong urge to go to sleep but it was a comparatively short journey and she told herself that she wasn't really tired.

'Do you often do this—get up in the night?'

'Quite frequently. I don't need much sleep.' He didn't tell her that he had only been in bed for a couple of hours when she had phoned. 'How will you manage at home?'

'Oh, I'll manage,' she assured him. 'We've got help from the village now I'm at the surgery, and there's not much to do.'

Which, considering the size of her home and her mother's helplessness, wasn't true.

'You'll be able to manage the surgery as well as household chores? I dare say your mother will help out.'

Leonora's reply to that sounded so doubtful that he didn't say any more.

Trotting behind the trolley bearing Nanny to her ward, Leonora was wide awake again; the doctor was talking to a solemn-looking man in a long white coat and appeared to have forgotten her; it seemed best to keep close to Nanny.

Waiting by the bed, she saw him coming towards her, still with the same man and this time with a nurse, who told her to wait outside the ward. 'There's a rest room, dear. We'll talk to you presently.'

It seemed a long time before James came looking for her.

'Come and see Nanny and then we'll go back,' he told her briskly. 'She's in good hands and there is an excellent chance of her recovery. She won't know you but don't let that worry you. We'll come and see her this evening.'

Nanny looked comfortable propped up on pillows, very small against them. She was dozing and although she didn't respond to Leonora's kiss it seemed as though she was better.

The doctor's hand on her arm roused her to say goodbye to the nurse and go with him back to the car, and he popped her in, got in beside her and drove away.

'I'll take you home,' he told her presently. 'You can do your hair and so on and I'll collect you in half an hour. You'll breakfast with me and we'll open the surgery at the usual time.'

'Oh, but I can't—I mean, there's breakfast to get for Mother and Father.'

'I dare say your mother will manage that for once,' he observed. 'You've a day's work ahead of you, remember.'

'So have you.'

'Ah, but I have Cricket to cosset me. And he will enjoy cosseting you too.'

'Yes, that would be nice, but...'

'Dear girl, will you do as I say?' He sounded so kind that she could have wept—just because she was tired and chilly and hungry.

She said, 'Yes, James,' in such a meek voice that he glanced at her in surprise.

At the house he went in with her, but there was no sound. He left her in the hall, reminding her that he would return in half an hour, and she went to her room, showered and dressed again, did her hair in its usual chignon and made up her tired face. There was just time to go to the kitchen, put the kettle on and lay a tray for early-morning tea. Wilkins, roused from sleep, went out into the garden, and she went upstairs to wake her parents.

There wasn't time to do more than give a quick explanation.

'I'll be back at lunchtime,' she told them. 'Wilkins has been out and you'll only have breakfast to get.'

Lady Crosby sat up in bed. 'My dear child, I'll do my best. You know I always do, however poorly I feel.'

'I dare say I can boil an egg,' said her father gruffly. 'Pity about Nanny.' He sipped his tea. 'I'll ring the hospital later. Is she very ill?'

'Yes, Father. I must go; I'll come home as soon as I can.'

She reached the door at the same time as the Rolls came to a silent halt before it. James got out and opened her door for her.

'You look as fresh as a daisy,' he observed. 'Parents awake?'

'Yes. Father said he'd phone the hospital later on.'

'I shall be going to see her this evening. Want to come with me?'

'Oh, yes.' He watched her tell-tale thoughts racing across her face. 'What time? I mean, I'll have to get a meal.'

'Put something in the oven. We shan't be away long. We'll go directly after surgery.'

Cricket had the door open as they reached it and she was marched straight into the dining room, her nose twitching at the delicious smells coming from the open kitchen door. She was sat down, given a cup of coffee and then, urged by her host, fell to on bacon, eggs, mushrooms and fried bread, and then, again gently persuaded by the doctor, toast and marmalade and more coffee.

She could have curled up in a chair and slept then but she was whisked out into the garden and walked briskly round while Tod circled about them. It was a cool, bright morning and by the time they had to leave for the surgery she was wide awake again. Cricket, handing her her jacket with a fatherly air, actually smiled widely.

'That was the most delicious breakfast,' she told him, and gave him a smile to melt his elderly heart.

She thanked James too with an even sweeter smile and he, a man who prided himself on his self-control, nodded casually, so that her heart, which had been thumping happily in his company, plunged into her shoes. But what do I expect? she thought, getting into the car once again.

# CHAPTER NINE

THERE weren't many patients at the surgery; by eleven o'clock the place was empty and Leonora put the kettle on and got out two mugs and the coffee. Dr Galbraith's round was smaller than usual too—she had looked in the book to check that—so it was disappointing when he declined a drink and went away with a brisk, 'I'll see you at this evening's surgery.'

After he had gone, she had her coffee, got the patients' notes out ready for the evening, took a few phone calls and tidied the place, then sat down to wait for Mrs Crisp. She arrived punctually and Leonora explained hurriedly about Nanny.

'The poor dear,' said Mrs Crisp warmly. 'But there, she's not all that young, is she? And that great house to manage—just the two of you. I don't know how you do it; let me know if I can be of any help, Miss Leonora.'

Leonora thanked her and made for the door, to be stopped by Mrs Crisp's voice. 'I almost forgot—you've not had time to see the local paper, of course. The doctor's advertising for a receptionist—part-time, like you. I dare say you want to get back to your usual...' She paused and added awkwardly, 'What I mean is, I dare say Sir William isn't too keen on your working here in the village. The doctor did tell me you were just helping out until he could get someone to suit him. He asked me if I'd like the job full-time but of course I haven't the time for that, so he says, "Well, Mrs Crisp, you stay on

167

part-time, and I'll find someone as soon as possible."'
She smiled. 'He's a real gentlemen, isn't he?'

Leonora said brightly, 'I hope he finds someone—
we're a bit out of the way, aren't we?' She smiled too.
'I must go; I'll be back on time.'

Perhaps it was a good thing she had no time to think
once she got home. Her mother was in the kitchen, opening and shutting drawers and cupboards in an aimless
way. 'Darling, here you are. I can't find anything, silly
little me. Will you make a salad for lunch, and perhaps
a cheese soufflé…?'

'Has Father phoned the hospital?' asked Leonora, dis-
missing the soufflé.'

'He thought it would be better to wait for an hour or
so, darling. By then Nanny may be feeling better.'

Leonora went back into the hall and picked up the
phone. Nanny was about the same, holding her own, she
was told, and she could ring again that evening if she
wished.

She went back to the kitchen. 'Where's Father,
Mother?' she asked, and began opening drawers and
cupboards, assembling lunch.

'In his study, dear. What shall we do about dinner this
evening?' Lady Crosby sat down. 'Oh, dear, I am so
upset…'

They had their lunch in the kitchen, which, Lady
Crosby observed, took away every vestige of her appetite. 'I think I'd better go and lie down for a while; I've
got one of my headaches coming on.'

Sir William helped to clear the table and Leonora said,
'I'm going to the hospital this evening with Dr Galbraith,
Father. I'll get everything ready for supper and I'm sure
Mother could manage if I'm not back. We're going di-
rectly after surgery.'

'Yes, yes, of course. I'll drive over in a day or so when Nanny feels more the thing!' He added uneasily, 'You're sure you can manage? I'm afraid your mother isn't up to doing much.'

'It isn't for long, Father, and I can manage.' She hoped she could; if and when Nanny came home, she would have her hands full. Perhaps the district nurse would help out. Time to worry about that later. There certainly wasn't time to worry now: beds to make, rooms to tidy, a tea-tray to set ready, a meal to prepare for the evening.

She arrived back at the surgery feeling tired and not looking her best

The doctor, seeing this and saying nothing, wondered how best to help her; the wish to carry her off to Buntings and keep her there was hardly practical. Besides, he had had no indication that she would agree to that. It was a problem he had no time to solve at the moment.

Later, as he drove past her home, she cast a guilty look at the lighted windows. Her mother and father would be coping as best they could; she ought to be there looking after them.

James had seen her glance. 'They'll cope,' he told her easily. 'It will be only for a short time and both your mother and father are very fit for their age—and they are by no means old.'

'Old?' She sounded shocked. 'Mother's in her early fifties; she married very young.'

'There you are, then.' He began to talk about something else and when they reached the hospital took her straight to Nanny.

Nanny looked as though a puff of wind would blow her away, but at least she recognised them.

'Such a botheration,' she wheezed, 'me feeling poorly; your ma will never manage.' She peered up at Leonora's face. 'And you'll be worked to death.'

'No, no, Nanny, we're managing beautifully. You aren't to worry. It's only for a little while anyhow. You'll be back home in no time.'

The doctor, standing beside her, made no effort to contradict this statement. Presently he wandered away to speak to the house physician.

'He's a good man,' said Nanny between coughs. 'Tell your ma and pa not to come visiting me; there's no need. Getting the best of treatment—such nice girls the nurses are; nothing's too much trouble.' She glanced at the flowers Leonora had brought with her. 'They'll look a treat on my locker. Now don't you waste your time coming here, Miss Leonora; you've enough on your plate.'

'If Dr Galbraith gives me a lift, it's the easiest thing in the world,' said Leonora. 'Is there anything you want, Nanny—books or magazines?'

'Bless you, no.' Nanny stopped to cough; she was tired now and Leonora said quickly, 'I'm going now, but I'll be back. Take care!'

She bent to kiss her old friend and left the ward to stand about outside its doors wondering where the doctor had gone. He joined her presently.

'I've had a talk with the man in charge of Nanny. She's doing well, even after twelve hours. Not quite out of the woods yet... She was pleased to see you!'

Leonora nodded. 'Yes, she was bothered about looking after Mother and Father.' She added, 'She looks very ill...'

'She is ill but the tests which have been done are all satisfactory; give the antibiotics a chance and she'll be as good as new.'

He spoke in a manner which she couldn't help but believe; she went with him to the car feeling cheerful, ready to cope with the evening ahead.

At the house he got out of the car and helped her out, but when she asked him to go in with her he refused. 'I'm dining out,' he explained. 'I'll see you in the morning. Don't worry about Nanny; she will be all right.'

She went indoors then, after thanking him politely for the lift and saying that she hoped he would have a pleasant evening—something which she hardly expected to have herself. And nor did she; there was too much to do.

Back from his dinner party later that evening, the doctor went in search of Cricket.

'I need your help,' he told him. 'This is what I want you to do...'

So the following morning Cricket made his stately way to the Dowlings' residence and remained closeted with Jenks, their butler, for some time.

'Oh no account must Miss Crosby be told that these come from Dr Galbraith; tell Sir William that Mr Dowling sent them as a gift. They're quite ready to be put into the oven...'

Jenks nodded a bald head. 'I'll see that's done, but why the secrecy, or may I not ask?'

'I'm not at liberty to say more, but shall we just say that there may be wedding bells in the offing? Strictly between us, of course. Nothing said, I fancy—the doctor isn't a man to hurry and Miss Crosby needs a delicate hand. A charming young lady, I must add, but touchy about money matters; I gather there's not much of it up at the house. Any whiff of charity and she would retreat.'

When Leonora got home at lunchtime she was met by her mother.

'Darling, such luck—the Dowlings have sent over a brace of pheasants they can't use. Ready to pop into the oven too. Isn't that marvellous? Now you'll have almost no cooking to do this evening.'

Leonora, who had been cudgelling her brains as to how to present sausages disguised as something else, was relieved at the news.

Evening surgery wasn't busy, which was a good thing, for the doctor was called away as his last patient was preparing to leave—Mrs Squires, complaining of aches and pains, demanding a bottle of tonic. There was nothing like it, she assured the doctor. 'And I dare say you may be a very clever man, but there's a lot you could learn about tonics.'

He agreed placidly, wrote out a prescription and left her in Leonora's hands, bidding them goodbye as he went.

A mean trick, thought Leonora, longing to get home to deal with the pheasants and delayed by Mrs Squires, eager for a nice long chat. By the time she did get home she was tired and cross; the pheasants still had to be dealt with...but first of all she phoned the hospital. Nanny was doing well, responding to the antibiotics, eating a little, sleeping well. She told her father and he agreed to drive over to the hospital on the following day.

'In the afternoon, Father,' urged Leonora. 'If we go directly after lunch we can be back in time for surgery.'

At morning surgery the doctor told her that he had talked to the house physician at the hospital. 'Nanny's doing well; they'll be sending her home in five or six days; can you manage?'

'Oh, easily,' said Leonora instantly, and added mendaciously, 'I've help from the village, you know.'

'Splendid. I shall be driving to the hospital this evening; do you want a lift?'

'Father's going this afternoon and I said I'd go with him. Thank you for the offer.'

Determined to preserve a cool front, she succeeded in sounding frosty instead.

Later, sitting in his study with Tod sprawled over his feet, James pushed aside the work he was doing and applied his powerful brain to the subject of Leonora's sudden coolness. What had he done or not done? he wondered. Surely she hadn't found out about the pheasants? If she had he was sure that she would have taxed him with that in no uncertain terms. She was avoiding him and although she was tired and worried her distance was caused by even more than that—something was making her unhappy.

Surely she wasn't still in love with Beamish? With five sisters he was only too well aware of the vagaries to be encountered in the female. He wished very much to tell her of his love for her but if he spoke now he might ruin his chances...

As the days went by it was so obvious that Leonora was avoiding his company that he took care that they spent as little time together as possible. An outbreak of chickenpox kept him busy both in and out of the surgery, and though he drove her to see Nanny one evening he was careful to behave with detached friendliness. From Cricket he heard that the help from the village was quite inadequate, that Lady Crosby seemed unable to lift a finger round the house, that Sir William didn't seem to notice any shortcomings as long as he had his meals, and that there were lights showing at the house long after sensible people were in bed.

Nanny was to be sent home in two days' time; the

pneumonia had been banished but she was still in need
of rest, good food and attention. At the hospital Leonora
greeted the news with a cheerful face, casting aside
Nanny's anxious worries as to how they were to manage;
indeed, to hear her, one would have thought that she had
boundless help! The doctor said nothing until they were
in the car going home.

'I will arrange for the nurse to come each day and get
Nanny up and dressed, and again in the evening to settle
her back in bed.'

'There's no need...'

He said levelly, 'I must remind you that I am Nanny's
doctor, Leonora.'

'Oh, well, yes. Thank you.' She added in a stilted
manner, 'We do appreciate your care and kindness. How
long will it take Nanny to get quite well?'

'Ten days, two weeks. If she wishes to potter before
then there is no reason why she shouldn't, but it would
be best if she takes things very easily for another week.'

'I'll make sure of that.'

'I'll fetch her home on Sunday morning; perhaps you
will come with me?'

'Yes, please.' She thanked him again as he dropped
her off at the house.

She watched him drive away and then walked round
the house to the garden door with Wilkins beside her.
'It's no good, Wilkins,' she observed. 'Everything's
gone wrong, hasn't it? He's just the family doctor!'

He lived up to that for the next two days—always
kind and friendly and at the same time aloof.

On Sunday she got into the car, delighted to be with
James even if he was keeping her at a distance. But she
need not have worried; he kept up a steady flow of
cheerful talk and at the hospital went with her to the

ward to fetch Nanny, who was dressed and ready and pale with the excitement of going back home again.

Leonora sat in the back of the car with her, exchanging places with Tod, who sat motionless beside his master, and listened to Nanny's observations about the nurses and doctors, the food and the treatments. 'They were all very kind,' said Nanny, 'but, of course, it's not like home, is it?'

The doctor carried her indoors and up the staircase to her room, taking no notice of her protests. 'I shall come to see you in a day or two; mind and do exactly what Leonora says—a week doing nothing much, Nanny. After that you can resume your reign in the kitchen.'

He spent a short time with Sir William and Lady Crosby while Leonora got Nanny back into her bed for a rest. 'Nurse will come morning and evening for the next week,' he told them. 'Leonora will need some help until Nanny is on her feet again; she has been quite ill and must do nothing much for a while.'

'Of course not,' agreed Lady Crosby. 'You may be sure we'll take good care of her. You'll stay for coffee? I'm sure Leonora will make some.'

'Thank you, I won't stop, but if I may I'll take a look at Nanny before I go.'

Nanny was sitting up in bed telling Leonora where to put her clothes. She turned a shrewd eye on him as he went in. 'This child will be worn out looking after me and this blessed great place; it's time I was on my feet.'

He sat down on the side of the bed. 'Just stay quiet for a little longer, Nanny. I won't allow Leonora to get worn out. Nurse is coming to help you each day and you may get up and sit here and walk about the room, but no more.'

He glanced about him. It was a cosy room and quite

well furnished; someone had put flowers in a vase on
the little table near the bed and the place was warm. He
supposed that there was some kind of central heating,
although keeping a house this size even comfortably
warm must be a problem. Fortunately the weather was
mild. He bade her goodbye, told Leonora not to see him
out, and went away.

'Now that's the man for you,' said Nanny, twitching
her elderly nose. She hadn't been blind, watching the
pair of them behaving as though they'd only just met.
She closed her eyes, ready for a nap. She need not
worry; the doctor was a man to sort out his own problems, Leonora's with them too, of course.

The week went slowly by; Leonora went to and from
the surgery, presenting a smiling face when anyone
looked at her. After only four days she was tired already,
but things would get easier, she told herself, and the
nurse was a great help. Besides, Nanny was getting better each day; the doctor had been to see her that morning
and pronounced himself more than satisfied. As he'd left
he had asked Leonora if she was managing.

'Oh, yes. Thank you,' she had told him brightly, her
eyes daring him to ask any more questions.

The next evening, dining at Colonel Howes' house,
he was surprised to see Sir William and Lady Crosby
among the guests. He went to speak to them as soon as
he could. 'Is Leonora not with you?' he wanted to know.

'Well, Nanny can't be left and Leonora said she was
tired anyway; a nice quiet evening will do her good,'
Lady Crosby told him.

Dinner was barely finished when he told his host that
he had a night call to make. 'I'll slip away quietly,' he
said. 'Otherwise it might break up the evening.'

He went to his home first and found Cricket in the kitchen.

'Food, Cricket,' said the doctor. 'Something nice and quick to eat. I'll get a bottle from the cellar. What have we got?'

'Cold chicken, Parma ham, some of my pâté if you can make the toast. Egg custard. A salad, if I can have five minutes.'

Ten minutes later the doctor, with Tod beside him, was driving through the village. Turning into the gates, he saw that most of the downstairs lights were on and, bidding Tod be quiet, he got out of his car and walked round the house to the garden door. It wasn't locked and he went in, restraining Tod as Wilkins began to bark. The old dog came running down the passage but stopped barking when he saw who it was and the three of them went on to the kitchen.

Leonora had her back to them. 'What's up, Wilkins?' she asked, and turned round. The look on her face when she saw James brought a gleam to his eyes although he remained unsmiling.

His expression showed nothing of his thoughts. That she offered no beautiful picture bothered him not at all. She was lovely—the most beautiful girl in the world— even dressed as she was in a worthy dressing gown and a pinny tied around her waist. Her hair hung in an untidy plait and her make-up had long ago passed its best. She was mopping the kitchen floor and the mop dripped unheeded as she stood looking at him.

He said in a soothing voice, 'Hello—I hope I didn't scare you. I thought we might have supper together.'

'Supper?' She stared at him and then smiled. 'Mother and Father have gone out to dinner...'

'Yes, I know; I was there.'

'You've had dinner—'

'I wasn't hungry but I am now.' He put his basket down on the kitchen table, took the mop from her, swabbed up the puddle it had made, and took it and the bucket over to the sink.

Leonora looked down at her person. 'I got ready for bed but it was a chance to get the housework done. I'll go and dress.'

'No need. Take off that pinny and wash your hands. I'm going to lock the garden door.'

When he came back he unpacked the basket, took the champagne from its cooler and poured two glasses.

'Champagne,' said Leonora faintly, and took a reviving sip. Somehow everything was all right; she looked a fright but James didn't seem to mind. They were friends again; if only they could stay like that. Only she would have to be careful not to betray her feelings. He found knives and forks and plates, and set out the food, refilling her glass.

Champagne on a very empty stomach did wonders for her ego; with a sigh of delight she demolished the delicacies Cricket had provided and had another glass of champagne.

'Stay there; I'll make coffee if you tell me which cupboard to get it from.'

They had their coffee, and she, in a delightful haze, had no idea what they talked about; all she knew was that she was happy.

James was happy too but to propose to his Leonora when she was so delightfully bemused with champagne wouldn't do at all. He cleared the supper things away, washed the dishes and put everything away tidily, and Leonora, watching him, said on a slightly boozy giggle, 'You'll make a good husband, James.'

He had his back to her. 'I value your opinion, Leonora,' he told her. Then in a quite different voice he added, 'I'm going to see Nanny; then when I am gone you are to go straight to bed—I want your promise about that.'

She gave the tiniest of hiccups and he smiled a little. 'I promise.'

He went away, going quietly through the house, and presently returned.

'Nanny is awake and perfectly all right. Come with me to the door and lock it after me.'

At the door she stooped to caress Tod. 'Thank you for a lovely supper, and please thank Cricket too.' She smiled up at him and he bent his head and kissed her—a hard, quick kiss which took her breath—and then walked swiftly away.

She locked the door then and went back to the kitchen to settle Wilkins and put out the lights, all the while in a glow of happiness.

Upstairs she wandered into Nanny's room to say goodnight.

Nanny gave her a thoughtful stare. 'Didn't I say that's the man for you?' she wanted to know. 'Go to bed, and sweet dreams, my pet.'

So Leonora did just that.

She went to work still in a glow of happiness the next morning, and the doctor gave a sigh of relief at the sight of her face as she wished him a good morning. His Leonora had at last allowed her feelings to show…

There were a lot of patients but none of them were seriously ill; they finished a little early and Leonora went to put the kettle on, turning to smile at James as he came into the waiting room.

'An easy morning,' he observed. 'Nanny is going on well?'

'Yes. She is longing to get into the kitchen; I do wonder what she is doing when I am not there.'

She had spoken jokingly but he answered seriously, 'Well, that's soon remedied. I have a receptionist coming on Monday so you will not need to come to the surgery any more.'

Leonora went pale. 'Not come? You mean you are giving me the sack?'

'Yes.'

'You don't want me here any more?'

'No. Oh, you have been entirely satisfactory—I'm not sure what I would have done without your help—but you did know that it was a temporary arrangement.' He smiled and her unhappy heart did a somersault. He went on, 'I hadn't meant to say anything—not here—but perhaps you'll come to Buntings and have lunch with me—there will be time to talk.'

'What about?' she asked, and before he could answer she said, 'No, I'm afraid I can't; I have to go home. Besides, there is nothing to talk about.' She went on rather wildly, 'And even if there was I wouldn't want to hear it.'

He turned off the gas under the kettle. 'Then you will have to hear it now...' He took the phone up as it rang and stood listening.

'Lacock's Farm? I'll be with you as quickly as possible. Get an ambulance and the fire brigade.'

He put the phone down. 'Where is Lacock's Farm exactly? Somewhere close to Norrington Common? How far?'

'Four miles. Off the road; there's a cart track to the farm.'

He was in the surgery, putting things into his bag. 'A barn roof has collapsed; there were a number of children inside. They've got three out, injured; there are several more inside.'

He came back into the waiting room, sweeping her along with him. 'You'll have to show me the way.'

He locked the surgery door, urged her into the car and drove off.

'Take the first turn on the left about half a mile away,' said Leonora, and moments later she added, 'Here, the road narrows. The track's about a mile on the right.'

The Rolls ate up the mile at a speed which boded ill for anything coming the other way; she let out a breath as James turned into the track. The pace was slower now. 'The farm is only a few hundred yards ahead,' she told him. 'You can't see it for the trees. It's on the left.'

The farmyard was large, with the farmhouse on its farther side and outbuildings on two sides, and beyond the house was the barn, its collapsed roof in a vast, sprawling pile, thatch and bricks and cob-walls still crumbling slowly.

The doctor drove up to the house, got out and opened Leonora's door, picked up his bag and strode to the barn. There were several people there: a woman standing in tears with a little girl in her arms, two men and a young boy climbing over the rubble searching.

The woman saw them first. 'Miss Crosby—Doctor. Tracey's hurt—her arm—and little Tim and Jilly are over there; there's no one to look after them.'

'See what you can do,' said the doctor to Leonora, and went over to the men.

'Into the house, I think,' said Leonora, hoping she would remember at least some of her first-aid lessons. 'I'll get the other two.'

She went to where they sat huddled on the ground, thanking heaven to find that they were more frightened than hurt. They had bumps and scratches but once in the house, where she could see them properly, she could find no bad injury. She sat them side by side on the old-fashioned sofa in the living room and turned her attention to Tracey.

The little girl was weeping copiously, which Leonora hoped was a good sign, but one small arm hung awkwardly, swollen and already showing bruises. Leonora opened drawers and cupboards, found a dinner napkin and made a sling. A warm drink, she remembered—sweet tea.

She sat a shocked Mrs Lacock beside the two children, settled Tracey on her lap and went in search of the teapot. She was in luck; the pot stood keeping warm beside the stove and if the tea was stewed she didn't think it would matter. She found mugs, milk and sugar and hurried back to the living room.

'Can you help the children to drink this and have some yourself? I'm going to see if I can do anything...'

The yard was slippery; they had been muck-spreading and she had to scramble carefully to where the men were clearing away rubble from the far end of the barn. As she reached them she saw the doctor stoop, draw a child out of the ruins and bend over her for a moment. She fetched up beside him and he handed the child to her. 'Take her indoors, lie her flat and cover her—a broken leg and concussion, I think; I'll come as soon as I can.'

The child was unconscious; Leonora laid her on a rug at Mrs Lacock's feet. 'Keep an eye on her,' she begged, and made her way back to the barn.

They were carefully edging a boy out of the medley of beams and thatch and stone and this time the doctor carried him back to the house and laid him down carefully beside the girl. 'Stay with him,' he told Leonora. 'There's still another child.'

She did what she could, thankful in a way that the two children were unconscious, keeping them covered warmly, wiping their small, dirty faces, gently cleaning the cuts she could reach without moving them. The sound of the ambulances, followed by the deeper note of the fire engine, didn't come a moment too soon, for the children needed expert care and despite her first aid there was little she could do.

There was activity now, men coming and going, taking over from the men and boy and James, who came into the house and began to examine the children. The paramedics came with him and Leonora, sitting with one of the children on her lap, watched him. For the moment she had forgotten that he had no interest in her, had made it clear that they were no more than acquaintances, living in the same village; he was the man she loved and always would love, unflappable in disaster, knowing what to do, never raising his voice, kind...

She watched for what seemed a very long time while he worked on the unconscious little boy and girl, who were taken away in the ambulance just as a shout heralded the rescue of the last child. Another boy. In a still worse state, she guessed, covered in dust and bits of thatch and blood. It was a long time before James was satisfied that he was well enough to be taken to the hospital. She could only guess at the emergency treatment he had been given.

It was the turn of the three children with Mrs Lacock, who between them were suffering from shock, a small broken arm and bruises and who after careful examination were got into the third ambulance and sent after the others.

The police were there now and James went away to talk to them, and a policewoman came into the house, asked Leonora if she was all right and went to make tea for everyone. Presently James came back, rolling down his shirtsleeves and putting on his jacket.

'You're all right?' he wanted to know. He spoke very gently. She looked like a scarecrow, covered in dust and earth and blood, her hair with half the pins missing. He thought she had never looked so beautiful.

'We'll go home,' he told her, 'and get clean and have a meal.'

Leonora got to her feet and followed him out to the car and sat quietly while he phoned Cricket. 'Let Lady Crosby know that Leonora is coming back with me, will you? We need to clean up and eat.'

'No,' said Leonora. 'I wish to go home.' Everything came rushing back then. 'And I do not wish to go to the surgery or to your house ever again!' She added as an afterthought, 'Thank you.'

James started the car. 'Ah, yes, I was interrupted, wasn't I? You will at least hear me out before you blight our lives for ever. Don't expect me to say any more at the moment; this infernal track takes all my patience.'

As he swept into the village she said once more, 'I want to go home.'

For answer he turned into his own gates. 'This is your home—or will be very shortly.'

She sat very still, not looking at him. 'You sacked me this morning...'

'Well, of course I did, you silly goose.'

He got out and ushered her into the house and Cricket came to meet them, tut-tutting at the sight of them.

'Show Miss Crosby to a room and a bathroom, Cricket, will you? And see if you can find a dressing gown or something similar while someone fetches some fresh clothes for her from the house.'

She was led away up the stairs to a pretty room with an adjoining bathroom. 'Just you have a nice hot bath, miss,' said Cricket, sounding very like Nanny. 'I'll arrange for someone to fetch your things and put a gown in the bedroom for you. And there's a tasty lunch ready when you are.'

Leonora stood in the middle of the room and looked at him. If only he knew how delightful it was to be taken care of. She blinked away tears and smiled. 'Thank you, Cricket; I won't be long.'

There were bath salts, bottles of fragrant oil, the very best of soaps, vast sponges and a shelf of lotions. There wasn't time to wash her dusty hair but she gave it a good brushing and got into a towelling bathrobe. It trailed on the ground and she had to roll up the sleeves and it shrouded her from neck to ankles. She went downstairs and found the doctor, very correctly dressed, in dark grey worsted and a dignified tie.

'We will eat first, then we will talk,' he said, resisting a strong desire to take her in his arms there and then; she was still wary of him and still cross...

Tod pranced to meet her and she bent to pat him before sitting down in the chair James was holding for her, surprised to find that she was hungry. Certainly the lunch Cricket served them would have tempted her even if she had had no appetite at all, and despite her unease the doctor's calm voice, rambling on in a soothing manner about nothing much, did a great deal to restore her usual good sense.

So she had got the sack, she reflected, spooning up a

nice old-fashioned junket with clotted cream, but that was to be expected; she'd had no reason to expect otherwise, had she? And she had been warned: Mrs Crisp had told her about the advertisement. She wondered what the receptionist would be like. Young and clever, never keeping James waiting, highly efficient and pretty...

'You aren't listening,' said James. 'We will go into the drawing room, where you will clear your sadly muddled thoughts and listen to me.'

'I must go home,' said Leonora, striving for common sense.

'Have you forgotten what I told you just now?'

They had crossed into the drawing room and were standing by the door into the garden while Tod dashed in and out.

'No, no, of course not.' She looked up at him. 'Only I'm not sure what you meant.'

He took her in his arms. 'Then I will tell you, and I will repeat what I am about to say as often as necessary for the rest of our lives. I've fallen in love with you, my darling; I think I did that when we first met even if you weren't at your dignified best.' He smiled down at her. 'I love you, my dearest Leonora, and I want to marry you.'

She looked up at him with shining eyes. 'Oh, James— and I want to marry you too, only I thought that you didn't love me, or even like me very much, so I tried to stop loving you, only I couldn't...'

He kissed her then, gently. 'My dearest love. So you will marry me—and soon?'

'As soon as we can.' She paused to think. 'Well, I must have some clothes and Mother will want to arrange things, I expect. I wish we could just creep away and get married now.'

He kissed her again, this time in a manner to leave her breathless.

'Mother and Father and Nanny,' said Leonora presently. 'Who will look after them? And Mother will want me to have a big wedding and Father can't afford that... Oh, dear!'

James gathered her closer. He said with calm assurance, 'Will you leave everything to me, my darling?'

Leonora, looking up into his face and seeing the love in it and hearing his calm, assured voice, said at once, 'Yes, of course I will, James.'

She smiled at him, wanting him to kiss her again.

Which James duly did, to her entire satisfaction.

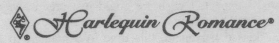
*Harlequin Romance®*

# Harlequin Romance® is proud to announce the birth of some very special new arrivals in:

BABY BOOM

## Because two's company and three (or more) is a family!

Our bouncing-babies series is back! Throughout 2000 we'll be delivering more bundles of joy, and introducing their brave moms and dads as they experience the thrills—and spills!—of parenthood!

Our first adorable addition is due in February 2000:

## THE BILLIONAIRE DADDY
### by Renee Roszel

Look out for other BABY BOOM romances from more of your favorite authors throughout 2000.

Available wherever Harlequin books are sold.

**HARLEQUIN®**
*Makes any time special.™*

# HEART OF THE WEST

# Every Man Has His Price!

Lost Springs Ranch was
famous for turning young
mavericks into good men.
So word that the ranch was
in financial trouble sent
a herd of loyal bachelors
stampeding back to
Wyoming to put themselves
on the auction block!

| | | | |
|---|---|---|---|
| July 1999 | *Husband for Hire*<br>Susan Wiggs | January 2000 | *The Rancher and<br>the Rich Girl*<br>Heather MacAllister |
| August | *Courting Callie*<br>Lynn Erickson | February | *Shane's Last Stand*<br>Ruth Jean Dale |
| September | *Bachelor Father*<br>Vicki Lewis<br>Thompson | March | *A Baby by Chance*<br>Cathy Gillen Thacker |
| October | *His Bodyguard*<br>Muriel Jensen | April | *The Perfect Solution*<br>Day Leclaire |
| November | *It Takes a Cowboy*<br>Gina Wilkins | May | *Rent-a-Dad*<br>Judy Christenberry |
| December | *Hitched by Christmas*<br>Jule McBride | June | *Best Man in Wyoming*<br>Margot Dalton |

## HARLEQUIN®
*Makes any time special* ™

Visit us at www.romance.net

PHHOWGEN